Adèle

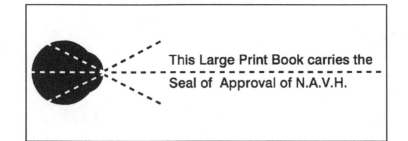

This Large Print Book carries the
Seal of Approval of N.A.V.H.

ADÈLE

LEILA SLIMANI

Translated from the French by Sam Taylor

WHEELER PUBLISHING
A part of Gale, a Cengage Company

Farmington Hills, Mich • San Francisco • New York • Waterville, Maine
Meriden, Conn • Mason, Ohio • Chicago

Originally published in French as *Dans le jardin de l'ogre* by Éditions Gallimard, Paris. English-language edition published simultaneously in the United States of America by Penguin Books and in the United Kingdom by Faber & Faber, Ltd.
Grateful acknowledgment is made to FTM Agency, Ltd., Russia for permission to quote from *Requiem* by Anna Akhmatova. Russian text copyright © by Margarita Novgorodova. English translation by Sacha Soldatow.
Quotations from *The Unbearable Lightness of Being* by Milan Kundera. English translation copyright © 1984 by Harper & Row, Publishers, Inc. Translated from *Nesnesitelná lehkost bytí,* copyright © 1984 by Milan Kundera. Reprinted by permission of HarperCollins Publishers.
Wheeler Publishing, a part of Gale, a Cengage Company.

**LIBRARY OF CONGRESS CIP DATA ON FILE.
CATALOGUING IN PUBLICATION FOR THIS BOOK
IS AVAILABLE FROM THE LIBRARY OF CONGRESS**

ISBN-13: 978-1-4328-5883-4 (hardcover)

Published in 2019 by arrangement with Penguin Books, an imprint of Penguin Publishing Group, a division of Penguin Random House LLC

Printed in Mexico
1 2 3 4 5 6 7 23 22 21 20 19

For my parents

It isn't me, someone else is suffering. I
   couldn't.
Not like this.

ANNA AKHMATOVA, *REQUIEM*

Vertigo is something other than the fear of
falling. It is the voice of the emptiness
below us which tempts and lures us, it is
the desire to fall, against which, terrified,
we defend ourselves . . . We might also
call vertigo the intoxication of the weak.
Aware of his weakness, a man decides to
give in rather than stand up to it. He is
drunk with weakness, wishes to grow even
weaker, wishes to fall down in the middle
of the main square in front of everybody,
wishes to be down, lower than down.

MILAN KUNDERA,
THE UNBEARABLE LIGHTNESS OF BEING

Adèle has been good. She has held out for a week now. She hasn't given in. She has run twenty miles in the past four days. From Pigalle to the Champs-Elysées, from the Musée d'Orsay to Bercy. In the mornings she has gone running on the deserted banks of the Seine. At night on the Boulevard de Rochechouart and the Place de Clichy. She hasn't touched a drop of alcohol and she has gone to bed early.

But tonight she dreamed about it and she couldn't fall back asleep. A torrid dream that went on forever, that entered her like a breath of hot wind. Now Adèle can think of nothing else. She gets up and drinks a strong black coffee. The apartment is silent. In the kitchen she hops about restlessly. She smokes a cigarette. Standing in the shower, she wants to scratch herself, to rip her body in two. She bangs her forehead against the wall. She wants someone to grab her and smash her skull into the glass door. As soon as she shuts her eyes she hears the noises: sighs, screams, blows. A naked man panting, a woman coming. She wishes she were just an object in the midst of a horde. She wants to be devoured, sucked, swallowed whole. She wants fingers pinching her breasts, teeth digging into her belly. She wants to be a doll in an ogre's garden.

She doesn't wake anyone. She gets dressed in the dark and does not say good-bye. She is too agitated to smile or have a conversation. Adèle leaves the building and walks the empty streets. Head down and nauseated, she descends the stairs of the Jules-Joffrin metro station. On the platform a mouse runs across her boot and startles her. In the carriage, Adèle looks around. A man in a cheap suit is watching her. He has badly shined shoes with pointed tips. He's ugly. He might do. So might that student with his arm around his girlfriend, kissing her neck. Or that middle-aged man standing by the window who reads his book and doesn't even glance at her.

She picks up a day-old newspaper from the seat opposite. She turns the pages. The headlines blur, she can't concentrate. Exasperated, she puts it down. She can't stay here. Her heart is banging hard in her chest, she's suffocating. She loosens her scarf, unwinds it from around her sweat-soaked neck and drops it in an empty seat. She stands up, unbuttons her coat. Holding on to the door handle, her legs shaken by tremors, she is ready to jump.

She's forgotten her phone. She sits down again and empties her handbag. A powder compact falls to the floor. She tugs at a bra strap entwined with earbuds. Seeing the bra, she tells herself she needs to be more careful. She can't have forgotten her phone. If she has, she'll have to go back home, come up with an excuse. But no, here it is. It was there all the time, she just didn't see it. She tidies her handbag. She has the feeling that everyone is staring at her. That the whole carriage is sneering at her panic, her burning cheeks. She opens the little flip phone and laughs when she sees the first name.

Adam.

It's no use anyway.

Wanting to is the same as giving in. The dam has been breached. What good would it do to hold back now? Life wouldn't be any better. She's thinking like a drug addict, like a gambler. She's been so pleased with herself for not yielding to temptation for a few days that she has forgotten about the danger. She gets to her feet, lifts the sticky latch, the door opens.

Madeleine station.

She pushes her way through the crowd that swells like a wave around the carriage and gushes inside. Adèle looks for the exit. Boulevard des Capucines. She starts to run. *Let him be there, let him be there.* Outside the storefront windows she hesitates. She could catch the metro here: Line 9 would take her directly to the office, she'd be there in time for the editorial meeting. She paces around the metro entrance, lights a cigarette. She presses her handbag to her body. Some Romanian women in head-scarves have spotted her. They advance toward her, holding out their stupid petition. Adèle rushes off. She enters Rue la Fayette in a trance, gets lost and has to retrace her steps. Rue Bleue. She types in the code and goes inside, runs upstairs to the second floor, and knocks on the heavy wooden door.

"Adèle . . ." Adam smiles. His eyes are puffy with sleep and he's naked.

"Don't speak." Adèle takes off her coat and throws herself at him. "Please."

"You could call, you know . . . It's not even eight yet . . ."

Adèle is already naked. She scratches his neck, pulls his hair. He doesn't care. He's hard. He shoves her violently, slaps her face.

12

She grabs his dick and pushes it inside her. Up against the wall, she feels him enter and her anxieties dissolve. Her sensations return. Her soul is lighter, her head an empty space. She grips Adam's ass and drives him into her angrily, ever faster. She is possessed, in a fever, desperately trying to reach another place. "Harder, harder," she screams.

She knows this body and that annoys her. It's too simple, too mechanical. Her surprise arrival did not transform Adam. Their lovemaking is not obscene enough or tender enough. She puts Adam's hands on her breasts, tries to forget that it's him. She closes her eyes and imagines that he's forcing her.

Already he is somewhere else. His jaw tenses. He turns her around. As always, he pushes Adèle's head down toward the floor with his right hand and grabs her hip with his left. He thrusts hard, he groans, he comes.

Adam tends to get carried away.

Adèle gets dressed with her back to him. She's embarrassed at him seeing her naked.

"I'm late for work. I'll call you."

"Up to you," replies Adam.

He smokes a cigarette, leaning against the kitchen door. With one hand, he touches the condom hanging from the end of his penis. Adèle looks away.

"I can't find my scarf. Have you seen it? It's gray cashmere. I'm really fond of it."

"I'll look for it. I can give it to you next time."

Adèle tries to act casual. The main thing is not to look as though you feel guilty. She crosses the open-plan office as if she's returning from a cigarette break. She smiles at her colleagues and sits at her desk. Cyril emerges from his glass cage. He has to shout to be heard above the din of keyboard rattle, phone conversations, chugging printers, and vending-machine discussions.

"Adèle, it's nearly ten!"

"I had a meeting."

"Yeah, right. You know what? You've missed your deadlines for two pieces, so screw your meeting. You've got two hours."

"Calm down, you'll get your articles. I'm almost done. After lunch, okay?"

"I've had enough of this shit, Adèle! We can't waste our time waiting for you. We've got a bloody paper to put out!"

Cyril is still waving his arms as he collapses on to his chair.

Adèle turns on her computer and covers her face with her hands. She has no idea what she's going to write. She should never have agreed to do this piece on social tensions in Tunisia. What the hell got into her, raising her hand in that editorial meeting?

She'll have to pick up the phone, call her contacts, ask questions, check facts, dig deeper. She'll have to care about her job, to believe in the journalistic rigor that Cyril is always going on about, that hypocrite who would sell his soul for a better circulation. She'll have to eat lunch at her desk, headphones over her ears, fingertips caressing her food-stained keyboard. To nibble at a sandwich while she waits for some self-important press officer to call her back and demand to read her article before it's published.

Adèle doesn't like her job. She hates the idea that she must work to make a living. The only ambition she ever had was to be looked at. She tried being an actress. When she first came to Paris she took classes, but apparently she lacked talent. The teachers said she had beautiful eyes and a certain mystery. "But to be an actress, mademoiselle, you must be able to let go." For a long time she stayed at home and waited for her destiny to reveal itself. Nothing went according to plan.

She would have loved being married to a rich, absent husband. To the outrage of all those proud working women who surround her, Adèle wishes she could spend her days lazing around a large house with no objective other than to look beautiful when her husband returns. How wonderful it would be to get paid for her talent of giving men pleasure.

Her husband makes a good living. A gastroenterology consultant at the Georges-Pompidou hospital, he works long hours and takes on extra shifts. They often go on vacation and they live in a large rented apartment in the eighteenth arrondissement. Adèle is spoiled and her husband is proud because he considers her a smart, independent woman. But it's not enough, she thinks. She finds her life small, shabby, lacking in grandeur. Their money smells of work, of sweat and long nights spent at the hospital. It has an aftertaste of reproachful looks and bad moods. It is not a passport to idleness or decadence.

Her husband pulled strings to get Adèle this job. Richard was friends with the son of the newspaper's managing editor and he put in a good word for her. That didn't bother her. It's just how the world works. To start with, she wanted to do a good job. She was excited by the idea of impressing her boss, surprising him with her efficiency and resourcefulness. She was bold and enthusiastic, landing the kind of interviews that no one else at the paper even dreamed about. Then she came to realize that Cyril was a thick-headed philistine incapable of appreciating her talent. She started to despise her colleagues, who drowned their failed ambitions in alcohol every night, and ended up hating her job, this office, this computer screen, the whole idiotic charade. She can no longer stand making phone call after phone call to ministers who refuse to comment before finally offering a few dull, hollow quotes. She is ashamed of the coquettish voice she puts on to win favors from a press officer. All that matters to her is the freedom the job gives her. Her salary is low but at least she gets to travel. She can disappear, invent secret rendezvous, without having to justify herself.

Adèle does not call anyone. She opens a blank document and starts to type. She invents quotes from high-up anonymous sources: "a figure close to the government," "a well-placed observer who asked to remain nameless." She comes up with a nice hook, adds a dash of humor to distract any readers who were expecting the article to provide some information. She reads a few other pieces on the same subject and copy-and-pastes lines from each. The whole thing takes her barely an hour.

"Here's your article, Cyril!" she calls out, putting on her coat. "I'm going for lunch — we can talk about it when I get back."

The street is gray and cold. The faces of the passersby are drawn, their complexions greenish. It all makes her want to go home and lie in bed. The tramp outside Monoprix is more drunk than usual. He's asleep on an air vent. His trousers are around his ankles and she can see his back and buttocks covered in scabs. Adèle and her colleagues enter a dirty little brasserie and, as always, Bertrand says, a bit too loud: "We weren't supposed to come back here, remember? The owner's in the National Front."

But they go there anyway, because it has a fireplace and the food is reasonably priced. To head off boredom Adèle makes conversation. She tells stories, asks her colleagues about their plans for Christmas, tries to rekindle old scraps of gossip. It's exhausting. The waiter comes over to take their order. When he asks what they would like to drink, Adèle suggests wine. Her colleagues look coy, halfheartedly shake their heads, claim they can't afford it. "It's on me!" Adèle announces, despite the fact that her bank account is overdrawn and these colleagues have never once bought her a drink. But so what? She's taking charge now, she's treating them, and after a glass of Saint-Estèphe, in the woodsmoke-scented air, she has the feeling that they love her and are forever in her debt.

It's three thirty by the time they leave the restaurant. They are slightly drowsy from the wine, the too-rich food, and the warmth of the fire that they can still smell on their coats and their hair. Adèle takes the arm of Laurent, whose desk is opposite hers. He is tall and thin and his cheap false teeth give him a horsey smile.

In the office, no one is working. The journalists doze behind their screens. Small groups talk at the back of the room. Bertrand teases a young intern who is imprudently dressed like a 1950s starlet. Champagne bottles are cooling on window ledges. Everyone is waiting until it's late enough to get drunk, far from their families and real friends. The newspaper's Christmas party is an institution: a moment of planned debauchery, where the aim is to go as wild as possible, to reveal your true self to colleagues with whom your relations will, the next day, become purely professional again.

None of her colleagues know this, but last year's Christmas party was a momentous one for Adèle. In a single night she fulfilled a fantasy and lost all professional ambition. In the editorial boardroom she slept with Cyril on the long black lacquered-wood table. They drank a lot that night, and she spent the evening close to him, laughing at his jokes and shooting him shy, sweet looks at every opportunity. She pretended to be both terribly impressed by and terribly attracted to him. He told her what he'd thought of her the first time he saw her.

"You looked so fragile, so shy and polite . . ."

"A bit uptight, you mean?"

"Yeah, maybe."

She licked her lips, very quickly, like a lizard. He was stunned. The newsroom emptied and, while the others picked up the plastic cups and cigarette stubs scattered over the floor, the two of them went upstairs to the boardroom. They threw themselves at each other. Adèle unbuttoned Cyril's shirt. She thought it looked so good on him when he was simply her boss and, in a sense, forbidden fruit. But now, on the black lacquered table, he was revealed as potbellied and clumsy. "Too much to drink," he said, to excuse his underwhelming erection. He leaned against the table, ran his fingers through Adèle's hair and pushed her head down between his thighs. With his dick touching the back of her throat, she repressed the urge to vomit and bite down.

And yet she had wanted him, before. She would wake early each morning to do her makeup, to choose a new dress, in the hope that Cyril would notice and perhaps even pay her a discreet compliment. She finished her articles well before deadline, suggested stories from all over the world, always arrived in his office with solutions and never problems, all of this with the sole intention of making him like her.

What was the point of working now that she'd had him?

Tonight Adèle keeps her distance from Cyril. She is sure that he's thinking about that night, but since then their relationship has grown very cold. She couldn't stand the ridiculous texts he sent her over the days that followed. When he shyly suggested one night that they go out to dinner, she just shrugged and said: "Why bother? I'm mar-

22

ried and so are you. It would only cause us pain, don't you think?"

Tonight Adèle has no intention of hitting the wrong target. She jokes around with Bertrand, who bores her with yet another description of his collection of Japanese manga. His eyes are red. He's probably just smoked a joint, and his breath is even more foul than usual. Adèle puts on a brave face. She pretends to enjoy the company of the obese female archivist, whose mouth — generally a source of grumbles and sighs — is shaped into a smile tonight. Adèle is starting to warm up. The champagne is flowing — a gift from a politician to whom Cyril recently devoted a flattering front-page story. She's getting restless. She feels beautiful and she hates the idea that her beauty will be wasted, that her good mood will be for nothing.

"You're not going home, are you? Let's go out! Come on . . ." she begs Laurent, who is chatting with three other journalists. Her eyes are shining and her voice is so full of enthusiasm that it would be cruel to refuse her anything.

"What do you think, guys?" Laurent asks his colleagues.

In the half-light, the window open on a view of pink clouds, Adèle observes the naked man. Face buried in a pillow, he is sleeping like a sated animal. He might just as easily be dead, like those insects that are killed by coitus.

Adèle gets out of bed, hands crossed over her bare breasts. She lifts the sheet from the man's sleeping body, which curls up to keep warm. She didn't ask him how old he was. His smooth skin, his plump flesh, and this attic room where he lives suggest that he is younger than he led her to believe. He has short legs and a woman's bottom.

The cold rays of dawn illuminate the disorderly room. Adèle gets dressed. She shouldn't have come here with him. At the very moment when they first kissed, his soft lips sticking to hers, she knew that she'd got the wrong man. He wouldn't be able to fill her. She should have fled then. Found an

24

excuse not to go up to this studio apartment. She should have said: "Well, we had fun, didn't we?" She should have left the bar without a word, pushing away those soft hands, that glassy gaze, that boozy breath.

She was too cowardly.

They staggered up the stairs. With each step the magic faded, her drunken joy giving way to nausea. He started to strip. She felt her heart shrink, faced with the banality of a zipper, the prosaic vulgarity of a pair of socks, the clumsiness of a drunk young man. She wished she could have said: "Stop, not another word. I don't want this anymore." But she felt cornered.

Lying beneath his hairless torso, all she could do was try to make it go quickly, simulating pleasure, overdoing the orgasmic moans so he would finish up, shut up, get it over with. Did he even notice that she had her eyes closed? She shut them in a rage, as if seeing him disgusted her, as if she was already thinking about the next men, the real men, the good ones, somewhere else, the ones who would finally know how to control her body.

She quietly opens the door of the apartment. In the building's inner courtyard she lights a cigarette. Three drags and then she calls her husband.

"I'm not waking you, am I?"

She tells him she spent the night at her friend Lauren's house, a few blocks from the newspaper office. She asks about her son. "Yeah, it was a good night," she says. Staring at the spotted mirror in the building's lobby, she smooths the lines around her eyes and watches herself lie.

In the empty street she hears her own footsteps. A man shoves past her as he runs to catch a slowing bus and she lets out a cry of alarm. To kill time she decides to walk home. She wants to be sure that she'll return to an empty apartment, where no one will question her. She listens to music and vanishes into the frozen city.

Richard has cleared away the breakfast things. The dirty cups are piled in the sink. There's a slice of toast stuck to one of the plates. Without taking off her coat, Adèle sits down on the leather sofa. She presses her handbag to her body. She doesn't move. The day will not start until she's taken her shower. Until she's washed the stale tobacco smell off her blouse. Until she's hidden the bags under her eyes with concealer. For now, she remains in her filth, suspended between two worlds, the mistress of the present tense. The danger is over. There is nothing more to fear.

Adèle arrives at the office, face drawn and mouth dry. She hasn't eaten since the previous night. She needs something in her stomach to soak up the dolor and the nausea. She bought a dry, cold pain au chocolat at the worst bakery in the neighborhood. She takes a bite of it but she can barely chew. She wants to roll up in a ball in the bathroom and go to sleep. She is exhausted and ashamed.

"Well, Adèle? Not too tired?"

Bertrand leans across his desk and winks at her, but she doesn't react. She tosses the pain au chocolat in the bin. She's thirsty.

"You were in top form last night! Not too hungover, are you?"

"I'm fine, thanks. I just need a coffee."

"You're like another person when you've had a few drinks, aren't you? Everyone sees you as this butter-wouldn't-melt little princess, but in fact you're a bit of a party animal!"

"Stop it."

"You gave us all a good laugh. And what a dancer!"

"Listen, Bertrand, I have work to do . . ."

"Me too, I've got loads of stuff to do. I barely slept at all. I'm exhausted."

"Well, good luck."

"I didn't notice you leaving last night. Did you go home with that guy? Did you get his name or was it just a one-nighter?"

"What about you — do you get the names of the whores you fuck when you're in Kinshasa?"

"Oh, calm down! I'm just messing with you. So your husband doesn't say anything when you get home at four in the morning, completely plastered? My wife gives me the bloody Spanish Inquisition . . ."

"Shut up!" Adèle cuts in. Breathing hard, cheeks bright red, she moves her face close to Bertrand's. "Never talk about my husband again, do you hear me?"

Bertrand draws back, both palms in the air.

Adèle is angry with herself for having been so reckless. She should never have danced, should never have been so open and approachable. She should never have sat on

Laurent's lap and told him, voice quivering, completely wasted, a sad story from her childhood. They saw her making out with that boy behind the bar. They saw her and they don't judge her for it, but somehow that makes it worse. Now they're going to think that she's available, that it's okay to be familiar with her. They're going to want to have a laugh with her. The men are going to think that she's up for it, easy, a slut. The women will treat her as a predator; the kinder ones might say that she's emotionally fragile. They will all be wrong.

On Friday night Richard suggests a trip to the beach. "We can leave early tomorrow. Lucien can sleep in the car." Adèle wakes at dawn so as not to upset her husband, who wants to avoid the traffic. She packs their bags, dresses her son. It's a cold, bright morning, the kind of day that clears the cobwebs from your head. Adèle is in a happy mood. In the car, perked up by the proud winter sun, she even makes conversation.

They arrive in time for lunch. The Parisians have colonized the heated terraces, but Richard was smart enough to make a reservation. Dr. Robinson leaves nothing to chance. He doesn't bother reading the menu: he knows what he wants. He orders white wine, oysters, whelks. And three sole meunières.

"We should do this every week! The sea air for Lucien, a romantic dinner for us . . .

It's perfect, isn't it? This feels so good, especially after the week I've had at the hospital. I didn't tell you this, but Jean-Pierre, the department head, asked me if I'd like to present a paper on the Meunier case. I said yes, of course. He owed me that. Anyway, I'm going to leave the hospital soon. I feel like I never get to see you and Lucien at the moment. The clinic at Lisieux has been back in touch — they're just waiting to get the green light. I've arranged to visit the house in Vimoutiers. We can see it while we're staying at my parents' place. Mom went to see it, and she says it's perfect."

Adèle has had too much to drink. Her eyelids are drooping. She smiles at Richard. She bites her cheeks to stop herself interrupting him and changing the subject. Lucien is fidgety — he's starting to get bored. He swings back on his chair, grabs a knife that Richard calmly takes from him, then he unscrews the top of the salt shaker and throws it across the table. "Lucien, that's enough!" Adèle scolds.

The child shoves his hand into his bowl and crushes a boiled carrot between his fingers. He laughs.

Adèle wipes her son's hand on a napkin.

"Shall we get the bill? This isn't fun anymore."

Richard pours himself another glass.

"So you didn't tell me what you thought about the house? I can't do another year at the hospital. Paris just isn't my scene. And you said yourself that you're bored out of your brains at the newspaper."

Adèle's eyes are fixed on Lucien, who fills his mouth with mint-flavored water and spits it out on the table.

"Richard, say something!" Adèle yells.

"What the hell is wrong with you?" Richard says, stunned. "Calm down! Everyone's staring at us."

"Sorry. I'm just tired."

"Can't you just enjoy the moment? Why do you have to spoil everything?"

"I'm sorry," Adèle repeats. She starts mopping up the paper tablecloth. "But Lucien's bored. He just needs to run around. If only he had a little brother or sister, and a big garden where he could play . . ."

Richard gives a conciliatory smile.

"What did you think of the ad? You liked that house, didn't you? As soon as I saw it I thought of you. I want us to change our life. I want us to *have* a life, you know what I mean?"

Richard puts his son in his lap and strokes his hair. Lucien looks like his father. The same fine blond hair, the same *calisson*-shaped mouth. They both laugh a lot. Richard is crazy about his son. Sometimes Adèle wonders if they even need a wife and mother. Perhaps the two of them could live perfectly happily without her.

She looks at them and realizes that her life will always be the same now. She will look after her children, worry about what they're eating. She will go on holidays to places that they like, try to find ways of entertaining them every weekend. Like bourgeois mothers the world over, she will drive them to their guitar classes, to the theater, to school, constantly seeking activities to "elevate their minds." Adèle hopes that her children will not be like her.

They go to the hotel and check in to their room, which is narrow and shaped like a boat cabin. Adèle doesn't like it. She has the feeling that the walls are slowly moving closer together, that they will crush her while she sleeps. But she does want to sleep. She closes the shutters on this beautiful day, puts Lucien down for his nap, and goes to bed. Barely has she closed her eyes when she hears her son calling her. She doesn't move. She is more patient than he is — he'll give up in the end. She hears small hands banging on a door and guesses that he's gone into the bathroom. He turns on the tap. "Take him out to play. We're only here for one day, poor kid. And I've just come off two days on duty."

Adèle gets up, dresses Lucien, and takes him to a little playground at the end of the beach. He climbs the brightly colored frames. He slides down the slide without ever getting bored. Adèle is afraid that he'll fall off the high platform where the children are jostling one another and she stands close to catch him if he does.

"Shall we go back to the hotel, Lucien?"

"No, Mommy, not yet," her son decides.

The playground is tiny. Lucien steals a toy car from a little boy, who starts crying. "Give that back to him. Come on, that's enough, let's go back to see Daddy," she begs, pulling at his arm. "No!" her son shouts. He runs toward the swings and almost smashes his jaw. Adèle sits on a bench then gets up again. "Why don't we go to the beach?" she suggests. He can't hurt himself on the sand.

Adèle sits on the cold beach. She puts Lucien between her legs and starts digging a hole. "We're going to dig a hole so deep that we'll find water. Watch!"

"I want the water!" Lucien cries out excitedly. After a few minutes he escapes and starts running toward the large puddles left by the retreating tide. The boy falls down, gets up again, and jumps into the muddy sand. "Lucien, come back!" Adèle shrieks. The boy turns around to look at her and laughs. He sits down in the puddle and plunges his arms into the water. Adèle does not get up. She is furious. It's December and he's going to be soaked. He'll catch a cold and then she'll have to look after him even more than she already does. She is angry with him for being so stupid, so thoughtless, so selfish. She thinks about getting up and dragging him back to the hotel, where she will demand that Richard give him a hot bath. But she doesn't budge. She has no desire to carry him, this boy who has grown so heavy and whose muscular legs kick her violently when he struggles. "Lucien, come here right now!" she yells. An old lady stares at her in shock.

A blond woman with a bad haircut, wearing shorts despite the cold, takes Lucien by the hand and leads him over to his mother. His jeans have ridden up over his chubby knees. He's smiling and embarrassed. Adèle is still sitting as the woman says in a strong

English accent: "I think this little one would like a bath."

"Thank you," Adèle replies, humiliated and anxious. She wishes she could lie flat on the sand, cover her face with her coat, and just give up. She doesn't even have the strength to shout at her son, who stands there shivering and smiling at her.

Lucien is a burden, a constraint that she struggles to get used to. Adèle isn't sure where her love for her son fits in among all her other jumbled feelings: panic when she has to leave him with someone else; annoyance at having to dress him; exhaustion from pushing his recalcitrant stroller up a hill. The love is there somewhere, she has no doubt about that. A rough, misshapen love, dented and bruised by everyday life. A love that has no time for itself.

Adèle had a child for the same reason that she got married: to belong to the world and to protect herself from other people. As a wife and mother, she is haloed with a respectability that no one can take away from her. She has built herself a refuge for her nights of anguish and a comfortable retreat for her days of debauchery.

She liked being pregnant.

Apart from the insomnia and the heavy legs, apart from the backache and the bleeding gums, Adèle had a perfect pregnancy. She quit smoking and drank only one glass of wine per month, and that healthy lifestyle was enough to fill her. For the first time in her life she had the impression that she was happy. Her swollen belly made her back arch gracefully. Her skin was radiant and she even let her hair grow, brushing it to one side.

By her thirty-seventh week it had become very uncomfortable to lie down. One night she told Richard to go out without her. "I can't drink. It's hot. I just don't see what I would do at that party. Go and have fun. Don't worry about me."

She lay down. The shutters were open and she could see the crowds walking in the streets below. After a while, unable to sleep, she got out of bed. In the bathroom she splashed cold water on her face and inspected her reflection for a long time. She looked down at her belly and then back up at her face. She wondered if she would once again become what she had been before. She was acutely aware of her own metamorphosis. She couldn't have said if this pleased her or if she was feeling nostalgic for the past. But she knew that something inside her was dying.

She had always thought that a child would cure her. She had convinced herself that motherhood was the only way out of her malaise, the sole solution that could end this perpetual flight from herself. She had thrown herself into it like a cancer patient finally accepting the necessity of chemotherapy. She had made this child — or, rather, this child had been made without any resistance from her — in the mad hope that it would be good for her.

No need for a pregnancy test. She knew straightaway, but she didn't tell anyone. She guarded her secret jealously. Her belly grew and she kept halfheartedly denying that she was going to have a baby. She was afraid that the people around her would ruin everything with their banal reactions, their vulgar gestures, touching the underside of her belly to feel its roundness. She felt alone, particularly with men, but that solitude didn't oppress her.

Lucien was born. She quickly started smoking and drinking again. The child stole her idleness and for the first time in her life she was forced to look after someone else. She loved that child. She loved him with an intense, physical love, but still it wasn't enough. Those days at home seemed endless. Sometimes she would let the baby cry in his crib while she covered her head with a pillow and tried to sleep. She would sob at the sight of the slimy, stained high chair, of this sad child who didn't want to eat.

She likes to hold his naked body tight against her before she puts him in his bath. She loves rocking him and watching him sink into sleep, drunk on her tenderness. Ever since his crib was swapped for a child's bed, she has slept next to him. Each night she noiselessly leaves the conjugal bedroom and slides under the covers beside her son, who grunts and turns over. She rubs her nose in his hair, against his neck, in the palm of his hand, sniffing his sour smell. She wishes so much that this would be enough to fill her.

Pregnancy ruined her. She has the impression that she came out of it ugly, soft, old. She cut her hair short and now her face seems to be riddled with lines. And yet, at thirty-five, Adèle is still a beautiful woman. Age has even rendered her stronger, more intriguing, more imperious. Her features have hardened but her pale gaze has grown more powerful. She is less hysterical, less excitable. Years of smoking have lowered the high-pitched voice that her father used to mock. Her pallor has become intense and you can almost trace the meanders of her veins now under her cheeks.

They leave the hotel room. Richard leads Adèle out by the arm. For a few minutes they remain frozen behind the door, listening to Lucien's howls as he begs them to come back. With a heavy heart they walk to the restaurant where Richard has reserved a table. Adèle had wanted to dress up but in the end she didn't bother. She was cold when she came back from the beach. She didn't feel like taking off her clothes, putting on the dress and the high-heeled shoes that she'd brought with her. It's just the two of them, after all.

They walk quickly along the street, side by side. They don't touch. They rarely kiss. Their bodies have nothing to say to each other. They have never felt any attraction or even tenderness for each other, and in a way this absence of carnal complicity is reassuring. As if it proves that their union is above all bodily contingencies. As if they have already mourned the loss of something that other couples part with reluctantly, amid tears and rows.

Adèle does not remember the last time she made love with her husband. Probably last summer. An afternoon. They have become used to all those arid nights when they wish each other sweet dreams and turn their backs. But still, a sense of embarrassment, a sourness, ends up disturbing the air around them. So Adèle feels a strange obligation to break this cycle, to offer her body to him once again so that they can then go on as they were before. For days on end she thinks about it as a sacrifice to which she must consent.

Tonight the conditions are in place. Richard's gaze is misty and a little bit ashamed. He's more clumsy than usual. He pays Adèle a compliment about how beautiful she looks. She suggests they order a good bottle of wine.

Over the first course Richard picks up the conversation where they left it at lunch. Between mouthfuls he reminds Adèle of the promises they made nine years ago when they got married. To enjoy Paris as long as their youth and their means allowed, then to move out when they had children. When Lucien was born Richard gave her a reprieve. "Two more years," she said. Those two years elapsed long ago and this time he is not going to give in. Hasn't she said dozens of times that she wants to quit her job, to devote herself to something else — writing, perhaps, her family? Haven't they agreed that they're tired of the metro, of traffic jams, of the high cost of living, of the whole damn rat race? Adèle says nothing. She barely touches her food. But Richard does not waver in the face of her indifference. He plays his last card.

"I'd like another child. A little girl — wouldn't that be wonderful?"

The alcohol has already stolen Adèle's appetite; now she wants to vomit. She has the impression that her stomach has swollen, that it's about to overflow. The only thing that could bring her relief is to lie down, not to move a muscle, to let sleep carry her away.

"You can finish my food if you want. I've had enough."

She pushes her plate toward Richard.

He orders a coffee. "Are you sure you don't want anything?" He accepts the Armagnac that the restaurant owner offers him on the house, and continues talking about children. Adèle is furious. The evening seems endless. If only he would change the subject . . .

Richard is a little drunk. On the way back to the hotel he makes Adèle laugh by suddenly breaking into a run. They enter their hotel room on tiptoe. Richard pays the babysitter. Adèle sits on the bed and slowly takes off her shoes.

He won't dare.

And yet he does.

There's no mistaking it. Always the exact same moves.

He comes up behind her.

The kiss on her neck.

The hand on her hip.

And then that murmur, that little moan, accompanied by a pleading sigh.

She turns around, opens her mouth, and her husband sticks his tongue inside it.

No foreplay.

Let's get it over with, she thinks as she undresses alone on her side of the bed.

They get in bed again. Bodies pressed together. Kissing constantly, as if it's real. She puts her hand on his waist, then on his penis. He penetrates her. She closes her eyes.

She doesn't know what Richard likes. What turns him on. She's never known. There is no subtlety to their lovemaking.

45

The years have not brought them closer, have not diminished the embarrassment. His movements are precise and mechanical. Straight to the point. She doesn't dare try taking her time. She doesn't dare ask. As if the frustration were so violent that she might end up strangling him.

She makes no sound. It would be awful if she woke Lucien and he caught them in this grotesque dance. She puts her mouth to Richard's ear and moans a little bit to salve her conscience.

It's over already.

He gets dressed straightaway. Acts as if nothing happened. Turns on the television.

He has never seemed to care about the solitude in which he abandons his wife. She felt nothing, nothing at all. She just heard the sounds they made, like a toilet plunger: torsos sticking, genitalia bumping.

And then, a vast silence.

Adèle's friends are beautiful. She was never stupid enough to surround herself with women less pretty than she is. This way, she doesn't have to worry about attracting unwanted attention. She met Lauren during a press trip in Africa. Adèle had just started at the paper and it was the first time she had accompanied a minister on an official tour. She was nervous. On the runway at Villacoublay, where a government airplane was waiting for them, she immediately noticed Lauren: six feet tall, backcombed platinum hair, face like an Egyptian cat. Lauren was already an experienced photographer, an African specialist who had been to every city on the continent and who lived alone in a studio apartment in Paris.

There were seven of them on the plane. The minister, a guy without any real power but whose career had been dramatic enough — corruption allegations, political turnarounds, sex scandals — to make him an important person. A jaunty technical adviser, probably an alcoholic, always ready with a smutty anecdote. A discreet bodyguard. A very blond and very chatty press officer. A skinny, ugly, chain-smoking journalist, famed for his rigor and the prizes he'd won, who regularly wrote front-page stories for his daily newspaper.

On the first night, in Bamako, she slept with the bodyguard. Drunk, and turned on by Adèle's desire, he danced topless in the hotel nightclub, his Beretta stuck in his belt. On the second night, in Dakar, she sucked off the adviser to the French ambassador in the toilets after slipping away from a deathly dull cocktail party where French expatriates blissfully rubbed shoulders with the minister while devouring canapés.

On the third night, on the terrace of the seaside hotel in Praia, she ordered a caipirinha and started joking around with the minister. She was about to suggest a midnight dip when Lauren sat next to her. "We should take some nice photos tomorrow — what do you think? It could help you with your article. Have you started it yet? Have you chosen an angle?" When Lauren asked her if she wanted to go up to her room to see a few photos, she thought they were going to sleep together. Adèle decided that she wouldn't be the man: that she would let the photographer lick her pussy but she wouldn't return the favor.

Her breasts, maybe. Yes, she might touch her breasts: they looked soft and welcoming. She had no qualms about tasting those breasts. But Lauren did not get undressed. She didn't show Adèle her photographs either. She lay on the bed and started talking. Adèle lay next to her and Lauren stroked her hair. With her head on the shoulder of this woman who was quickly becoming her friend, Adèle felt exhausted, completely empty. Before falling asleep, she suddenly sensed that Lauren had saved her from some calamity and she felt an immense gratitude toward her.

Tonight Adèle is waiting on Boulevard Beaumarchais, outside the gallery where her friend's photographs are being exhibited. She warned Lauren: "I'm not going inside until you get there."

She forced herself to attend. She would have preferred to stay at home, but she knows that Lauren is angry with her. They haven't seen each other for weeks. Adèle has canceled several dinner dates at the last minute, she's found excuses not to go out for a drink. Her guilty feelings are amplified by the fact that she has so often asked her friend to cover for her. She's sent her texts in the middle of the night: "If Richard calls, don't answer! He thinks I'm with you." Lauren has never answered any of Richard's calls, but Adèle knows she has become unhappy about playing this role.

In reality Adèle has been avoiding her. The last time they saw each other, for Lauren's birthday, she had decided to be on her best behavior, to be a perfect and generous friend. She helped her prepare the party. She took care of the music and even bought bottles of Lauren's favorite champagne. At midnight Richard went home so that their babysitter wouldn't have to stay too late.

Adèle was bored. She roamed from group to group, abandoning conversations in the middle of a sentence, incapable of focusing on anything. She started laughing with a man in an elegant suit and asked him, eyes shining, to pour her a drink. He hesitated. He looked around nervously. She did not understand his embarrassment until his wife arrived, furious, and vulgarly announced: "Settle down, all right? This one's married!" Adèle laughed mockingly and replied: "I'm married too. You have nothing to worry about." She moved away, chilled and trembling. She smiled to cover up the emotion she felt at being attacked by that bitchy woman.

She took refuge on the balcony, where Matthieu was smoking a cigarette. Matthieu was the great love of Lauren's life. He'd been her lover for the past ten years, feeding her on illusions that she still believed — that one day he would marry her and they would have children together. Adèle told him about the incident with the jealous wife and he said he understood why other women were afraid of her. They stared into each other's eyes. At two in the morning he helped her to put on her coat. He offered to drive her home and Lauren said, in a disappointed voice: "Oh yes, I forgot you were neighbors."

After driving a few yards, Matthieu parked in a street off Boulevard du Montparnasse and undressed her. "I always wanted to." He grabbed Adèle by the hips and put his mouth between her legs.

The next day Lauren called her. She asked if Matthieu had mentioned her, if he'd said why he didn't want to spend the night at her place. "You were all he talked about," Adèle replied. "You know perfectly well that he's obsessed with you."

■ ■ ■ ■

A wave of winter jackets spurts out of the Saint-Sébastien Froissart metro station. Woolly hats, lowered heads, department store bags swaying from the hands of mothers and grandmothers. In the trees the small discreet Christmas baubles look as if they're freezing to death. Lauren waves. She is wearing a long white cashmere coat, soft and warm. "Come on, there are lots of people I want you to meet," she says, dragging Adèle by the arm.

The gallery consists of two adjoining rooms, both quite small, with a buffet hastily assembled between them: drinks in plastic cups, chips and peanuts on paper plates. The exhibition is devoted to Africa. Adèle barely even stops in front of the photographs of packed trains, dusty towns, laughing children, and dignified old people. She likes Lauren's pictures, taken in the scrublands of Abidjan and Libreville, of couples embracing, covered with sweat, drunk on dancing and banana beer. Men in short-sleeved shirts, khaki or pale yellow, hold the hands of voluptuous girls with long braided hair.

Lauren is busy. Adèle drinks two cups of

champagne. She is restless. She has the feeling that everyone is staring at her because she's alone. She takes her phone from her pocket and pretends to send a text. When Lauren calls out her name, she shakes her head and shows her the cigarette that she's holding between gloved fingers. She doesn't feel like answering questions about what she does for a living. She is bored at the mere thought of all these penniless artists, these journalists pretending to be poor, these bloggers who have opinions about everything. The idea of making conversation is unbearable. Just being there, tasting the night, losing herself in banalities. Going home.

Outside, a damp and ice-cold wind burns her face. The weather probably explains why there's only one other smoker out there on the sidewalk: a short man with reassuringly broad shoulders. His narrow gray eyes meet Adèle's. She stares at him confidently, without lowering her gaze. Adèle swallows a mouthful of champagne and her tongue feels dry. They drink and they talk. A conversation about nothing very much, full of knowing smiles and easy insinuations. The best kind of conversation. He pays her compliments, she laughs softly. He asks for her name, she refuses to tell him, and this gentle, banal mating dance makes her feel alive again.

All their words are mere preliminaries for this moment, now, in this deserted back alley, where Adèle is pressed against a green Dumpster. He's ripped her tights. She lets out little moans, throws her head backward. He slides his fingers inside her, rubs his thumb on her clitoris. She closes her eyes so she doesn't have to meet the gaze of any passersby. She grabs the man's soft, slender fist and shoves it into her. He starts to moan too, abandoning himself to the unexpected desire of an unknown woman, one Thursday night in December. Excited, he wants more. He bites her neck, pulls her toward him, and starts to unzip his fly. His hair is messed up and his eyes are wide now. He looks like one of those starving men in the gallery's photographs.

She steps back, smooths down her skirt. He pats down his hair and collects himself. He tells her he lives close by — "near Rue de Rivoli." She can't. "That was good, thanks."

Adèle walks back to the gallery. She is afraid that Lauren has already left, afraid of having to go home alone. She spots the white coat.

"Ah, there you are."

"Lauren, walk me home. You know it scares me. You don't mind walking on your own at night. You're not afraid of anything."

"Come on, then. Give me your cigarette."

They walk, clinging together, along Boulevard Beaumarchais.

"Why didn't you go with him?" Lauren asks.

"I have to go home. Richard's expecting me. I told him I wouldn't be late. No, I don't want to go that way," she says abruptly as they arrive at Place de la République. "There are rats in the bushes. Rats as big as little dogs. I'm serious!"

They stick to the Grands Boulevards. The night sky darkens and Adèle grows nervous. Alcohol makes her paranoid. All the men are staring at them. Outside a kebab shop three men yell out "Hey, girls!" and make her jump. Gangs of men surge from nightclubs and an Irish pub, staggering, laughing, with an edge of aggression. Adèle is frightened. She wishes she were in bed with Richard. The doors and windows closed. He wouldn't let anyone hurt her, he would defend her. She walks faster, pulling Lauren by the arm. She wants to get home as fast as possible, to be at Richard's bedside, in the warm calm of his gaze. Tomorrow she will make dinner. She'll clean the house, she'll buy flowers. She'll drink wine with him and tell him about her day. She'll make plans for the weekend. She will be conciliatory, gentle, servile. She'll say yes to everything.

"Why did you marry Richard?" Lauren asks, as if reading her thoughts. "Were you really in love with him? I can't understand how a woman like you could have ended up in this situation. You could have kept your freedom, lived your life the way you want to, without all these lies. It just seems . . . absurd."

Adèle looks at Lauren in surprise. She cannot grasp what her friend is saying to her.

"I married him because he asked me. He was the first one, the only one so far. He had things to offer me. And anyway, my mother was so happy. I mean, he's a doctor!"

"Are you serious?"

"I don't see why I should have to stay alone."

"Independent isn't alone."

"Like you, you mean?"

"Adèle, I haven't seen you in weeks and you can't have spent more than five minutes with me tonight. I'm just an alibi for you. The way you behave . . ."

"I don't need an alibi. If you don't want to do me a favor, I'll find another solution."

"You can't go on like this. You'll get caught. And I've had enough of trying to look poor Richard in the eye while I tell him a load of lies."

"Taxi!" Adèle rushes into the road and a car stops. "Thanks for walking with me. I'll call you."

Adèle enters the lobby of her apartment building. She sits on the stairs, takes a new pair of tights from her handbag, and puts them on. She rubs her face, neck, and hands with wet wipes. She arranges her hair. She goes upstairs.

The living room is in darkness. She is grateful to Richard for not waiting up for her. She takes off her coat and opens the bedroom door.

"Adèle? Is that you?"

"Yes, go back to sleep."

Richard turns over. He reaches out across the empty bed, trying to touch her.

"I'll be there in a minute."

He hasn't closed the shutters, and when she gets into bed Adèle can see the peaceful expression on her husband's face. He trusts her. It's as simple and as brutal as that. If he woke, would he see the night's traces on

57

her? If he opened his eyes, if he got close to her, would he smell a suspicious scent, would he sense her guilt? Adèle hates him for his naïveté, which persecutes her, which deepens her sin and makes her even more despicable. She wants to scratch that smooth, tender face of his, rip apart this reassuring bed.

And yet she does love him. He is all she has in the world.

She convinces herself that tonight was her last chance. That she won't do it again. That from now on she will sleep in this bed with a clear conscience. It won't matter how closely he looks at her, there'll be nothing to see.

Adèle slept well. With the duvet pulled up to her chin, she tells Richard that she dreamed about the sea. Not the old, greenish sea of her childhood, but the real sea: lagoons, rocky inlets, umbrella pines. She was lying on a hot, hard surface. A rock, perhaps. She was alone. Carefully, shyly, she took off her bra. Squinting, she turned toward the open sea, and thousands of stars — fragmented reflections of the sun on the water — prevented her from opening her eyes wide. "And in the dream, I thought to myself: Remember this day. Remember how happy you were."

She hears her son's footstep on the floorboards. The bedroom door opens slowly and Lucien's round, puffy-eyed face appears. "Mommy," he whines, rubbing his eyes. He gets in their bed and, though usually so fidgety, so reluctant to hug, he rests his head on Adèle's shoulder. "Did you sleep well, my love?" she asks gently, very carefully, as if afraid that the slightest wrong note might spoil this moment of grace. "Yes, I slept well."

She gets up, with the boy in her arms, and walks over to the kitchen. She feels exhilarated, like an impostor whose true identity has not yet been exposed. Full of gratitude for being loved and paralyzed by the idea of losing everything. At this moment nothing seems more precious to her than the reassuring sound of the electric razor at the end of the hallway. Nothing seems worth endangering these mornings with her son in her arms, this tenderness, this need he has for her and that no one else will ever have. She makes pancakes. Quickly changes the tablecloth that she's left on the table for the past week despite the yellow stain at its center. She makes coffee for Richard and sits down next to Lucien. She watches him bite into the pancake and suck his jam-smeared fingers.

While she waits for her husband to come out of the bathroom, she unfolds a sheet of paper and starts writing a list. Things to do, most of which should have been done long ago. Her head is clear now. She is going to clean up her life. One by one, she is going to jettison her anxieties. She is going to do her duty.

When she arrives at the newspaper, the office is almost deserted. Clémence is the only one present, and she seems to live here. She always wears the same clothes anyway. Adèle pours herself a coffee and tidies up her desk. She throws out the stacks of printed articles, the invitations to events that have already happened. In little green and blue folders she files away all the documents that seem interesting, but which she will of course never look at again. With her mind uncluttered and her conscience appeased, she starts work. She counts out "One, two, three" to overcome her reluctance to call people, then picks up the phone and starts dialing numbers. "Try again later." "Ah, no, you'll have to ask that in writing." "What? Which newspaper? No, I have nothing to say." She keeps hitting a wall, but she doesn't give up. Each time, she goes back into battle, rephrasing the questions that they refuse to answer. She is persistent. When she can't write anymore, she walks through the long corridor that leads to a small inner courtyard. She goes out to smoke a cigarette, notes in hand, and repeats out loud her intro and her payoff.

By four o'clock the piece is finished. She's

smoked too much. She's not satisfied. In the editorial meeting everyone is animated. Cyril is thrilled. "Nothing like this has ever happened in Tunisia. I'm telling you, it's going to get worse. This will end in blood." She is about to send her article to the editor when her phone starts to vibrate. The white phone. She digs around at the bottom of her handbag. Opens it. A text:

"Adèle, I can't stop thinking about you, about that magical night. We have to see each other again. I'll be in Paris next week — we could go for a drink or for dinner, whatever you prefer. It can't end here. Nicolas."

She immediately deletes the message. She is furious. She met that guy a month ago at a symposium in Madrid. The journalists were there just to drink the free alcohol and enjoy their luxury hotel rooms paid for by a mysteriously funded think-tank. About three in the morning she followed Nicolas into his room. He had a hook nose and very nice hair. They had sex, stupidly. He kept pinching and biting her. She didn't ask him to wear a condom. True, she was drunk, but she let him sodomize her without a condom.

The next morning, in the hotel lobby, she treated him coldly. She didn't say a word in the car that took them to the airport. He seemed surprised, disconcerted. He didn't appear to understand that he disgusted her.

She gave him her number. Without knowing why, she gave him the number for her white phone, which she usually reserved for the men she wanted to see again. Suddenly, she remembers that she told him where she lived. They talked about her neighborhood and he even said: "I love the eighteenth."

Adèle doesn't feel like going to this dinner party. She had trouble choosing an outfit, always a bad sign. Her hair is dull and dry, her skin paler than ever. She locks herself in the bathroom and replies in a drab voice when Richard asks her to hurry up. Behind the door she can hear him chatting with the babysitter. Lucien is already asleep.

In the end Adèle dresses in black. She never used to wear black when she was younger. Her wardrobe was wild and fanciful, all reds and bright oranges, all lemon-yellow skirts and electric-blue heels. As her spark faded with age, she came to prefer darker shades. These days she wears bold jewelry over her gray sweaters and black turtlenecks.

Tonight she has gone for a pair of men's trousers and a sweater cut low in the back. She highlights her green eyes — the color of a Japanese pond — with turquoise eyeliner. She puts lipstick on and then wipes it off. A reddish trace remains around her mouth, as if someone has just greedily kissed her. Through the door she hears Richard gently ask: "Are you nearly ready?" She knows that he is smiling at the baby-sitter as if to say: "Ah, these women . . ." Adèle is ready but she wants him to wait for her. She spreads a towel on the bathroom floor and lies down. She closes her eyes and hums a melody.

Richard keeps talking to her about Xavier Rançon, the man to whose house they are invited. Xavier is a brilliant surgeon, the latest in a long family line of famous doctors. "A guy with an ethical code," Richard stresses. To keep him happy, Adèle replies: "I'm looking forward to meeting him."

The taxi drops them in front of a pair of gates guarding a private driveway. "Classy!" Richard enthuses. Adèle too is impressed by the place's beauty, but she would rather die than let her emotion show. She shrugs. He pushes open the gate and they walk up the paved path to the front door of a narrow three-story villa. The new owners have kept the art deco architecture while adding a floor with a large plant-filled terrace.

Adèle smiles shyly. The man who opens

the door leans toward her. He is stocky and wears a too-tight white shirt tucked into his jeans. "Hello, Xavier."

"Hello, I'm Sophie," says the mistress of the house.

Adèle offers her cheek in silence.

"I'm sorry, I didn't catch your name," Sophie says in a voice like a teacher's.

"Adèle."

"This is my wife," Richard says. "Good evening."

They climb the wooden stairs and enter a vast living room with two taupe sofas and a 1950s Danish table. Everything is oval-shaped and immaculate. An immense black-and-white photograph of a derelict Cuban theater decorates the back wall. A candle on a shelf radiates the reassuring scent of a luxury boutique.

Richard goes over to the men, who are sitting at the bar. They talk in loud voices, laugh at corny jokes. They rub their hands as they watch Xavier pour them glasses of Japanese whiskey.

"Something to drink?" Sophie suggests to the women who surround her.

Adèle holds out her glass. She looks over at the men and tries to find a way out, some excuse that will allow her to leave this group of squawking parakeets. These women are nothing. She does not even feel any desire to impress them. It is killing her to have to sit here and listen to them.

". . . So I said to Xavier, listen, darling, if we want this extra floor, we should do it! Sure, it's three months of work, but look at the result: we're in the middle of Paris and our villa has a living room like a cathedral! . . . The building work? Oh, it was a nightmare! It's a full-time job, you know. Thankfully I wasn't working. We're so glad that we bought, though . . . It's such a shame to waste thousands of euros on renting, don't you think? The square footage? About 110,000. Incredible, isn't it?

"What? The children? Oh, they've been asleep for hours! We're quite strict about their bedtime, so they didn't wait up for you. I would have liked you to see them, though — they've grown so much . . . Marie-Lou plays the violin and little Arsène is starting to eat real food now. We found a really great girl to look after them. She's African, very nice, and she speaks good French . . . Yeah, she's got her papers. I wouldn't mind hiring an illegal immigrant to clean the house, but not to look after my children. Never. That would be irresponsible. The only problem is that she observes Ramadan, and, you know, I just don't get that. You can't look after children when you're starving, can you? No, you're right, it's not reasonable. But I'm hoping she'll figure it out for herself and just stop. And what about you, Adèle, what do you do?"

"I'm a journalist."

"Oh! That must be interesting!" Sophie exclaims, pouring more wine into the glass that Adèle holds out. She looks into her eyes and smiles, as if encouraging a timid child to speak up.

"Well, dinner's ready. Shall we move to the table?"

Adèle pours herself more wine. Xavier, who is sitting to her left, takes the bottle from her hand and apologizes for not having served her. The other guests laugh at Richard's jokes. Adèle doesn't think he's funny at all. She can't understand why he's the center of attention.

Anyway, she's not listening anymore. She is bitter and irritable. Tonight she seems unable to exist. No one sees her, no one hears her. She doesn't even try to suppress the images that flash through her mind, that burn behind her eyelids. Her leg shakes beneath the table. She wants to be naked, she wants someone to touch her breasts. She wants to taste another mouth on hers, to feel a silent, animal presence. Her only ambition is to be wanted.

Xavier stands up. Adèle follows him to the bathroom, at the end of a narrow hallway. As he comes out she stands in his way and rubs past him, sensing his unease. He goes back to the dining room without turning around. She enters the bathroom and stands in front of the mirror, moving her lips while smiling, miming a polite conversation with herself. Her mouth is dry and purple.

She sits back down and puts her hand on Xavier's knee. He quickly moves his leg away. She can sense his determination to avoid her gaze. She drinks to give herself more courage.

"You've got a little boy, Adèle?" Sophie asks.

"Yes. He'll be three next month."

"How wonderful! And what about the next one? When do you think that will be?"

"I don't know. Probably never."

"Oh no! An only child? That's so sad. When I think about the happiness a brother or sister can bring, I could never deprive my children of that."

"Adèle thinks children are too time-consuming," Richard jokes. "But once we're in our new house, with more space and a big garden, I think she'll change her mind.

You'll want to fill it with children, won't you, darling? We'll be moving to Lisieux next year. I've been offered a fantastic opportunity to be a partner in a clinic!"

It's all she can think about now. Being alone with Xavier, just for five minutes, there at the end of the hallway where you can hear the echo of conversations from the living room. She doesn't find him handsome, or even attractive. She doesn't know what color his eyes are, but she is sure that she would feel relieved if he slid his hand under her sweater and then under her bra. If he pushed her against the wall, if he rubbed his erection against her, if she could sense that he desired her as much as she desired him. They couldn't go any further, they'd have to be quick. She'd have time to touch his dick, perhaps even get on her knees to suck him off. They'd start laughing, then return to the living room. They wouldn't go any further and that would be perfect.

Sophie is an unattractive woman, thinks Adèle, staring at her hideous necklace. A string of yellow and blue plastic beads held together by a silk ribbon. She is a boring woman, Adèle convinces herself, an idiotic parakeet. She wonders what that kind of woman — an ordinary woman — is like in bed. She wonders if she knows how to feel or give pleasure, if she says "make love" or "fuck."

In the taxi home Richard is tense. Adèle knows that he's annoyed. That she is too drunk, that she made a spectacle of herself. But Richard says nothing. He leans his head back, takes off his glasses, and closes his eyes.

"Why do you keep telling everyone that we're moving out of Paris?" Adèle goads him. "I never agreed to that, but you act like it's a fait accompli."

"You don't want to move?"

"I didn't say that either."

"So you haven't said anything. You never do say anything, in fact," he observes calmly. "You never tell me what you want, so you can't blame me for making a decision. And seriously, I don't know why you feel the need to behave like that. To get drunk. To talk down to people as though you alone understand the mysteries of the world and we are just a bunch of moronic sheep. You know, you're just as ordinary as we are, Adèle. The day you finally accept that, you'll be a lot happier."

The first time Adèle visited Paris she was ten years old. It was during the autumn half-term holidays and Simone had booked a room in a small hotel on Boulevard Haussmann. For the first few days she left Adèle alone in the room. She made her swear not to open the door to anyone, under any circumstances. "Hotels are dangerous places, especially for a little girl." Adèle had wanted to tell her: "Don't leave me on my own, then." But she didn't.

On the third day Adèle lay down under the thick duvet of the big hotel bed and turned on the television. She watched evening fall through the little window that overlooked a gloomy, gray courtyard. The sky outside was black and her mother still hadn't returned. Adèle tried to sleep, lulled by the laughter and advertising jingles emitted by the television. She had a headache. She had lost all notion of time.

Though desperately hungry, she didn't dare take anything from the minibar, which her mother had told her was a "rip-off." She rummaged around in her backpack in search of a chocolate bar or the remains of a ham sandwich, but all she found were two boiled sweets with scraps of tissue paper stuck to them.

She was falling asleep when she heard a knock at the door. She didn't answer it, but the knocks kept coming, harder and more insistent. Adèle approached the door. It had no spyhole. She couldn't see who was behind the door and she didn't dare open it. "Who's there?" she asked in a trembling voice. There was no response. The knocking grew louder and she heard footsteps in the hotel corridor. She had the impression that she could hear a sigh, a long, hoarse sigh, an irritated sigh that would end up lifting the door off its hinges.

She was so frightened that she hid under the bed, covered in sweat, convinced that her assailants were going to come in and find her there, crying into the beige carpet. She thought about calling the police, shouting for help, screaming until someone came to her aid. But she was incapable of moving, her legs jelly, her head spinning.

By the time Simone opened the door,

about ten o'clock, Adèle had fallen asleep. Her foot was sticking out from under the bed and Simone grabbed her by the ankle.

"What are you doing under there? What nonsense have you been up to now?"

"Mommy! You're here!" Adèle crawled out and jumped into her mother's arms. "Someone tried to come in! I hid. I was so scared."

Simone held her by the shoulders and examined her attentively. In a cold voice she said: "You were right to hide. That's exactly what you should have done."

The day before they left Paris, Simone kept her promise to take Adèle on a tour of the city. A man came with them, though Adèle cannot remember his name or his face. All she recalls is his musky tobacco smell and her mother's tense, nervy voice when she commanded Adèle to "say hello to the gentleman."

The gentleman took them to eat lunch in a brasserie near Boulevard Saint-Michel and gave Adèle her first taste of beer. They crossed the Seine and walked to the Grands Boulevards. Adèle dawdled in front of the toyshop windows in Passage Verdeau, Passage Jouffroy, and Galerie Vivienne, ignoring Simone's impatient nagging. Then they went to Montmartre. "The kid'll like that," the gentleman kept repeating. At Place Pigalle they took a tourist train and Adèle, wedged between her mother and the man, stared with terror at the Moulin Rouge.

Her memories of that visit to Pigalle are dark and frightening, at once murky and terribly vivid. True or not, she remembers seeing dozens of prostitutes on Boulevard de Clichy, half-naked despite the November drizzle. She remembers gangs of punks, swaying junkies, pimps with slicked-back hair, pointy-breasted transsexuals in skin-tight leopard-skin skirts. Protected by the bumps and jolts of this giant toy of a train, squeezed between her mother and the man, who kept shooting each other lascivious looks, Adèle felt for the first time that mix of fear and longing, disgust and arousal. That dirty desire to know what was happening behind the doors of those seedy hotels, in the dim depths of those back alleys, in the seats of the Atlas Cinema, in the back rooms of sex shops whose pink and blue neon signs pierced the twilight. Never since that evening — not in the arms of men, nor during the walks she took years later on the same boulevard — has she ever rediscovered that magical feeling of actually touching the vile and the obscene, the heart

of bourgeois perversion and human wretch-
edness.

For Adèle the Christmas holidays are a cold, dark tunnel, a punishment. Because he is generous and good, because he values family above all else, Richard has promised to take care of everything. He's bought the presents, had the car serviced, and, yet again, found a wonderful gift for Adèle.

She needs a holiday. She's exhausted. Not a day passes without someone telling her how thin she looks, how drawn, how moody she seems. "The fresh air will do you good." As if the air in Paris were less fresh than elsewhere.

Every year they spend Christmas in Caen with the Robinson family and the New Year with Adèle's parents. It has become a tradition, as Richard likes to repeat. She has tried to convince him that it is pointless to go all the way to Boulogne-sur-Mer to see her parents, who couldn't care less anyway. But Richard insists, for Lucien, "because he needs to know his grandparents," and for her too, "because family is important."

The house where Richard's parents live smells of tea and soap. Odile, his mother, rarely leaves her enormous kitchen. Sometimes she comes to sit in the living room, smiles at the guests who are there for aperitifs, starts a conversation, then vanishes back to her sanctuary of saucepans. "Come on, Mom, just stay here," pleads Richard's sister Clémence. "We came here to see you, not to eat," she always repeats, while wolfing down slices of toast loaded with foie gras and cinnamon biscuits. She always offers to help her mother, promises that she will take care of tomorrow night's dinner. And then, to the great relief of Odile, she sinks into an endless nap, often too drunk to recognize the ingredients of the main course.

The Robinsons are excellent hosts. Richard and Adèle are greeted with the sounds of laughter and popping champagne corks. A huge Christmas tree stands in the corner of the living room. The tree is so tall that its top touches the ceiling and bends back, giving the impression that it might collapse at any moment. "It's ridiculous, that tree, isn't it?" Odile chuckles. "I told Henri it was too big but he insisted on having it."

Henri shrugs and holds his hands apart in a gesture of helplessness. "I'm getting old . . ." He gazes in acknowledgment at Adèle with his blue eyes, as if the two of them shared some affinity, were members of the same tribe. She leans toward him and kisses his cheek, filling her nostrils with his smell of grass and shaving cream.

"Dinner's ready!"

The Robinsons eat, and when they eat they talk about food. They swap recipes, names of restaurants. Before the meal Henri goes into the cellar to unearth bottles of wine that are met with great *ah*s of excitement. Everyone watches him unscrew the cork, pour the nectar into a carafe, inspect its color. Then there is silence as Henri pours a dash of wine into a glass and sniffs its bouquet. He tastes it. "Ah, my children . . ."

At breakfast, when the kids eat sitting on their parents' laps, Odile looks deeply serious. "All right, you must tell me," she says slowly. "What do you want to eat for lunch?" "Whatever you like," Richard and Clémence invariably reply, used as they are to their mother's ways. At noon, while Henri opens the third bottle of this "very drinkable little Spanish wine," while their mouths are still full of the taste of pâté or cheese, Odile gets up and, notebook in hand, laments: "I have no inspiration for tonight's menu. What do you fancy?" No response but a few tired murmurs. Slightly drunk, desperate to take a nap, Henri sometimes gets annoyed with his wife. "We haven't even finished lunch and already you're bothering us about dinner!" Odile falls silent and sulks like a teenager.

This endless routine amuses and irritates Adèle in equal measure. She does not understand this polite hedonism, this obsession everyone seems to have with "eating well" and "drinking well." She always liked being hungry. Feeling herself bend but not break, hearing her stomach groan emptily and then conquering her need, proving herself above all that. Thinness has become a way of life.

Tonight, as usual, dinner lasts forever. Adèle has eaten almost nothing, but no one has mentioned this fact. Odile has given up trying to force-feed her daughter-in-law. Richard is tipsy. He's talking politics with Henri. They call each other fascists, bourgeois reactionaries. Laurent tries to insinuate himself into the conversation.

"Par contre . . ."

"En revanche," Richard interrupts. *"Par*

contre is incorrect. You should say *en revanche.*"

Adèle puts her hand on Laurent's shoulder, gets to her feet, and goes upstairs to her bedroom.

Odile always gives them the yellow bedroom, the largest and quietest in the house. It's a slightly gloomy room, with a very cold floor. Adèle gets in bed, rubs her feet together, and sinks into a deathlike sleep. During the night she sometimes has the impression of being half-awake. Her mind is on standby but her body is as rigid as a corpse. She senses the presence of Richard beside her. She has the agonizing sensation that she will never be able to rouse herself from this lethargy. That she will never wake from these bottomless dreams.

She hears Richard taking a shower. She perceives the time that has passed, guesses that it must be morning. Lucien's voice, the distant clatter of saucepans from the kitchen below, reach her ears. It is late but she doesn't have the strength to get up. Just five more minutes, she tells herself. Another five minutes and then the day can begin.

When she emerges from the bedroom, puffy-eyed and sweating, the breakfast table has already been cleared. Richard has left her a plate in the kitchen. Adèle sits down in front of her coffee. She smiles at Odile, who sighs: "I've got so much to do today, I don't know how I'm going to cope."

Adèle looks through the bay window at the garden. The big apple trees, the drizzle, the children speeding down the wet slide in their winter coats. Richard is playing with them. He's wearing his boots. He signals to Adèle that she should join them. But it's too cold. She doesn't want to go out.

"You're very pale," Richard says when he comes in. "You don't look well." He reaches out with his hand toward her face.

Henri and Clémence insisted on going to visit the house. "I want to see it. You know the locals call it the manor?" Odile practically pushed them out the door, delighted to be left alone to organize the Christmas festivities. Laurent volunteered to look after the children.

Richard is nervous. He berates Clémence for taking too long to get in the car. He makes his father promise not to say anything during the visit. "I ask the questions, understood? You keep your opinions to yourself." Adèle sits in the back, calm and indifferent. She looks at Clémence's fat thighs spread across the seat, her bitten-down nails.

Richard keeps turning around. Even though she tells him to watch the road, he can't stop looking at her, trying to discover what impression this country road is having on her. What does she think of those misty hills, this steep path, that wash house down there? What does she think of the entrance to the village? Of that church, sole survivor of the bombardments during the war? Can she see herself walking, day after day, amid these hillsides with their twisted apple trees? In these valleys with their streams, on this little track that leads to the house? Does she like this ivy-covered wall? Expressionless, her face glued to the window, Adèle refuses to say a word. She barely even blinks.

Richard parks the car outside the wooden gate. Mr. Rifoul stands waiting for them, hands behind his back like the lord of the manor. He's a giant of a man, obese and red-cheeked. His hands are as big as a child's face. His feet look as if they are about to sink into the ground. His thick, curly hair used to be blond and is now turning white. From afar he is impressive, but as they approach him Adèle notices his long fingernails. The missing button in the middle of his shirt. A dubious stain on the crotch of his trousers.

The owner extends his arm toward the front door and they enter the house. Richard bounds like a puppy up the front steps. As they visit the living room, kitchen, and veranda, he keeps interjecting little *ah yes*es and *excellent*s. He asks about the heating and the state of the electrical wiring. He checks his notebook and says: "Any leaks?" Between the living room — with its French windows looking out on a beautiful garden — and the old kitchen, Mr. Rifoul takes them into a little room that has been turned into an office. He opens the door reluctantly. The room has not been cleaned for a long time and dust motes dance in a dense crowd in the ray of sunlight that escapes between the blue curtains.

"My wife was a big reader. I'll be taking the books with me. But I can leave you the desk if you like." Adèle stares at the hospital bed against the wall with its neatly folded white sheets. A cat is hiding under the armchair. "By the end, she couldn't get out of bed."

They climb a wooden staircase. There are photographs of the dead woman on all the walls, smiling and beautiful. In the master bedroom, whose windows frame the view of an ancient chestnut tree, there's a hairbrush on the bedside table. Mr. Rifoul leans down and, with his massive hand, smooths the flower-patterned bedspread.

This is a house to grow old in, thinks Adèle. A house for tender hearts. It's made for memories, for friends who drop by and others who drift away. It's an ark, a clinic, a

85

refuge, a tomb. A godsend for ghosts. A theater set.

Are they really that old? Can their dreams truly end here?

Is it already time to die?

Outside, the four of them observe the facade. Richard turns toward the garden and waves his hand vaguely.

"How far does it go?"

"A long, long way. See that orchard over there? All that is yours."

"You'll be able to make apple tarts and compote for Lucien!" Clémence laughs.

Adèle looks down at her feet. Her polished loafers have been soaked by the wet grass. They are not shoes designed for the country-side.

"Give me the keys," she says to Richard.

She sits in the car, takes her shoes off, and warms her feet up with her hands.

"Xavier? How did you get my number?"

"I called your office. They told me you were on vacation, but I explained that it was urgent . . ."

She should tell him that she's glad to hear from him but that he shouldn't start getting any ideas. She is really sorry for the way she behaved the other night — it was wrong of her. She'd had too much to drink, she was a bit sad, she doesn't know what got into her. She's not that kind of person at all. Never in her life has she done anything like that before. He should forget about it, pretend it never happened. She's so ashamed. And anyway, she loves Richard, she could never do that to him, especially not with this man, Xavier, whom he is so proud to call a friend.

She doesn't say any of this.

"Is now a good time? Can you talk?"

"I'm at my parents-in-laws' house. But I

can talk, yes."

"How are you?" he asks in a completely different voice.

He tells her that he wants to see her again. That he was so aroused by her, he didn't sleep a wink that night. He only acted coldly because he was surprised — by his attitude toward her and her desire for him. He knows he shouldn't. He's tried to resist the urge to call her. He's done all he can to stop thinking about her. But it's no good: he has to see her.

Adèle says nothing. She smiles into the phone. Her silence embarrasses Xavier, who can't stop talking. In the end he asks if they could meet for a drink. "Wherever you want. Whenever you want."

"It's better if we're not seen together. How could I explain that to Richard?" She regrets saying this. He is going to realize that she is used to taking this kind of precaution.

But no. Instead he interprets this as a sort of deference, a desire that is nervous but determined.

"You're right. When you get back to Paris? Call me. Please."

She has bought a dark-red dress. A lacy dress with short sleeves, offering glimpses of her torso and her thighs. She slowly unfolds the dress on her bed. She tears off the label and pulls at a thread. She should have gone to fetch a pair of scissors but she couldn't be bothered.

She dresses Lucien in the shirt and leather shoes that his grandmother bought for him. Sitting on the floor with a toy truck between his legs, her son looks very pale. For the past two days he's been waking at dawn and refusing to nap. Eyes wide, he listens to the grown-ups' promises about Christmas Eve. At first amused, and then wearily, he submits to the blackmail that everyone practices on him. He is no longer fooled by the adults' vague threats. "If you're not good . . ." Just let Father Christmas come. Let's get it over with.

■ ■ ■ ■

At the top of the stairs she holds hands with her son, aware of Laurent's gaze fixed on her. As she descends he prepares to speak, to pay her a compliment on that provocative dress, and he stammers something that she doesn't hear. All evening long he takes photographs of her, using Clémence's obsession with making memories as an excuse. She pretends not to notice him staring at her through the lens of his camera. He thinks he's capturing chance moments of a cold and innocent beauty, but in fact every pose is calculated.

Odile sits in a chair near the Christmas tree. Henri fills flutes of champagne. Clémence cuts up bits of paper, and this year, for the first time, Lucien pulls the names from a bowl to decide who will receive their presents next. Adèle feels ill at ease. She wishes she could join the children in the dining room and lie down amid the Legos and toy strollers. She catches herself praying that her name will not be drawn.

But it is. "Adèle, ha!" they shout. They rub their hands and start a feverish dance around her chair. "Have you seen Adèle's gift?" Odile worries. "Henri, that little red parcel, have you seen it?"

Richard says nothing.

He sits on the arm of the sofa and waits for the perfect moment. Once Adèle's knees are submerged in scarves and mittens that she will never wear, cookery books that she will never open, Richard advances toward her. He hands her a box. Clémence looks reproachfully at her husband.

Adèle tears off the wrapping paper and when the little orange box appears with the black Hermès logo on it, Odile and Clémence sigh with satisfaction.

"You're mad. You shouldn't have." Adèle said exactly the same thing last year.

She undoes the ribbon and opens the box. To start with she doesn't understand what it is. A gold wheel decorated with pink stones and topped with a carving of three ears of wheat. She looks at the jewelry without touching it, without looking up and running the risk of meeting Richard's eye.

"It's a brooch," he explains.

A brooch.

She feels very hot. She's sweating.

"It's so beautiful," whispers Odile.

"Do you like it, darling? It's an old piece. I felt certain it would suit you. As soon as I saw it I thought of you. It's very elegant, don't you think?"

"Yes, yes. I like it a lot."

"So try it on. At least take it out of the box. Do you want me to help you?"

"She's emotional," says Odile, fingers gripping her chin.

A brooch.

Richard takes the object out of its box and presses on the pin, which lifts up.

"Stand up, it'll be easier like that."

Adèle stands and Richard delicately pins the brooch to her dress, just above her left breast.

"It doesn't go with this sort of dress, of course, but it's pretty, don't you think?"

No, of course it doesn't go with this kind of dress. She'll have to borrow a suit from Odile. A scarf too. She'll have to grow her hair and tie it up in a bun. She'll have to start wearing block-heeled shoes.

"Very pretty, my love. My son has excellent taste," Odile says proudly.

Adèle does not accompany the Robinsons to the midnight mass. She has a fever and she falls asleep in her garnet dress, curled up under the covers. "I knew you were getting ill," Richard laments. Even after he rubs her back and piles on extra blankets, she is still chilled to the bone. Her shoulders shake, her teeth chatter. Richard lies down next to her and holds her in his arms. He strokes her hair. He makes her take medicine the way he would Lucien, simpering a little bit.

He's often told her before that cancer patients, when they're dying, start to apologize. Just before they take their last breath, they ask forgiveness for sins that they have not had time to explain. "I'm sorry, I'm sorry." In her delirium Adèle is afraid to speak. She is wary of her weakness. Fearful that she will confide in whoever is looking after her, she uses the last remnants of her energy to bury her face in the drenched pillow. Say nothing. Whatever you do, say nothing.

Simone opens the door, a cigarette dangling from her lips. She is wearing a wrap dress, badly tied so it offers a glimpse of her dry, suntanned chest. She has thin legs and a round belly. Her teeth are stained with lipstick and, seeing this, Adèle can't resist the urge to rub her tongue against her own teeth. She examines the clumps of cheap mascara clinging to her mother's lashes, notes the blue pencil lines on her wrinkled eyelids.

"Richard, darling, I'm so happy to see you. I was so disappointed that you weren't coming to celebrate Christmas with us. Although it's true that your parents do know how to do things properly. We can't afford to be as chic as they are."

"Hello, Simone. We're very happy to be here, as always," Richard says enthusiastically as he enters the apartment.

"It's nice of you to say so. Get up, Kader,

can't you see that Richard is here?" she shouts at her husband, who is slumped in a leather armchair.

Adèle lingers on the threshold. She is carrying the sleeping Lucien in her arms. She glances at the blue chintz banquette and gets goose bumps. The living room looks even smaller and uglier than before. The black bookshelf opposite the sofa is cluttered with trinkets and photographs — of her and Richard, and of her mother when she was younger. A collection of matchboxes is gathering dust in a large saucer. Fake flowers are arranged in a Chinese-style vase.

"Simone, no smoking!" Richard scolds her, gently wagging his index finger.

Simone stubs out her cigarette and stands against the wall to let her daughter pass.

"I won't kiss you. We don't want to wake the little one, do we?"

"No. Hello, Mom."

Adèle walks through the tiny apartment and enters her childhood bedroom. She keeps her eyes fixed to the floor. She slowly undresses Lucien, who has opened his eyes but is not struggling for once. She puts him to bed. She tells him more stories than she usually does. He is sleeping deeply when she opens the last book but she continues to read, in a very soft voice, the story of a rabbit and a fox. The boy stirs and pushes her out of his bed.

Adèle walks through the dark hallway that smells of mildewed laundry. She joins Richard in the kitchen. He is sitting at the yellow Formica table and he shoots a complicit grin at his wife.

"Your son takes a long time to fall asleep," Simone says. "You spoil that kid. I never went in for any of that nonsense with you."

"He likes stories, that's all."

Adèle steals the cigarette from between her mother's fingers.

"You should have got here earlier. It'll be ten o'clock before we eat at this rate. It's a good thing Richard was here to keep me company." She smiles and nudges the bridge of her yellowed incisor with the tip of her tongue. "We've been very lucky to find you, Richard. It's a miracle, really. Adèle was always so awkward and prudish. Never a word, never a smile. We thought she'd end up an old maid. I kept telling her to make herself more attractive — men need to be seduced, after all! — but she was so stubborn, so secretive. I could never get her to confess anything. And there were plenty of blokes who had a thing for her . . . Oh yes, she was very popular, my little Adèle. Eh, weren't you, very popular? See? She doesn't even answer me. She's up on her high horse again. I told her: Adèle, get a grip on yourself! If you want to act like a princess, you'd better find yourself a prince because we can't afford to look after you. With your dad being sick and me slaving away all my life . . . I've got a right to enjoy myself too, you know! Don't be a fool like me, I told Adèle. Don't marry the first one who comes along and then spend the rest of your life regretting it. I used to be beautiful, Richard, did you know that? Have I shown you this picture before? It's a yellow Renault. The first in our village. And have you noticed that my shoes match my handbag? Always! I was the most elegant woman in the village. Ask anyone, they'll tell you. No, I'm very thankful that she found a man like you. Seriously, we've been very lucky."

Adèle's father is watching television. He has not got out of his seat since they arrived. He is engrossed by the New Year's Eve celebrations in Paris. His eyes stare out over swollen pouches, but they still contain a certain haughty spark. He still has a good head of hair for a man his age. It's brown, with a dusting of gray at the temples. His large forehead is still as smooth as ever.

Adèle sits next to him, her bottom hardly touching the banquette and her hands on her thighs.

"Do you like the television?" she asks in a very soft voice. "Richard chose it, you know. It's the latest model."

"It's very nice, love. You spoil me. You shouldn't spend your money on us."

"Do you want something to drink? They've started the aperitifs without us in the kitchen."

Kader moves his hand closer to Adèle and slowly taps her knee. His fingernails are shiny and smooth. They look very white next to his long tanned fingers.

"Leave 'em in peace, they don't need us," he whispers, leaning toward her. He smiles at her knowingly and takes a bottle of whiskey from under the table. He pours two glasses. "She always likes to show off in front of your husband. Well, you know your mother. She's spent her life organizing dinner parties to impress the neighbors. If I hadn't had her on my back, annoying me all the time, I'd have lived a real life. I'd have been like you. Living in Paris. Journalism — I bet I'd have liked that."

"We can hear you, Kader," Simone sniggers.

He turns back to face the television and squeezes his daughter's slender knee.

■ ■ ■ ■

Simone does not have a real dining-room table. Adèle helps her to set the plates on two little round low tables, each consisting of a bronze tray and wooden trestles. They eat in the living room, Kader and Adèle sitting on the banquette, Richard and Simone on small blue satin poufs. Richard has trouble concealing the discomfort of this seating arrangement. Handicapped by his six-foot-two-inch frame, he eats with his knees touching his chin.

"I'm going to check on Lucien," says Adèle.

She goes into the bedroom. Lucien is asleep, his head half hanging off the bed. She pushes his body against the wall and lies down next to him. She can hear the music from the television and she closes her eyes to silence her mother. She balls her fists. Now all she can hear is the rousing music and all she can see is the insides of her eyelids filled with stars and glitter. Gently she moves her arms and holds tight to the naked shoulders of the dancers on the television. She dances too, languorously, looking beautiful and ridiculous in a pink tutu like a circus animal's. She is not afraid anymore. She is nothing but a body, offered up for the pleasure of tourists and retirees.

The holidays are over. She is going back to Paris, solitude, Xavier. Finally she will be able to skip meals again, be silent, hand Lucien over to whoever will have him. Ten, nine, eight, seven, six, five, four, three, two, one: happy new year, Adèle!

Nothing went as planned. To start with, they couldn't find a car. Adèle was fifteen, Louis seventeen, but he had promised that one of his friends — an older kid who hung around outside school during classes — could take them to the beach in his father's car. On Sunday morning, though, there was no sign of this friend. "Never mind, we'll take the bus." Adèle said nothing. She didn't admit that her mother had forbidden her to use public transport, especially to leave the city, and especially with boys. They waited twenty minutes for the bus. Adèle was wearing skintight jeans, a black T-shirt, and one of her mother's bras. She had shaved her legs the night before in the little bathroom. She'd used a man's razor that she'd bought at the grocery store and she'd made a mess of it. Her legs were covered with scratches now. She hoped it wasn't obvious.

In the bus, Louis sat next to her. He put

his arm around her shoulders. He chose to talk with her rather than with his friends. He's treating me like I'm his woman, like I belong to him, she thought. She liked that.

The trip lasted more than half an hour and when they got to end of the line they had to walk for a while to reach the house belonging to Louis's friend, the famous beach house to which he'd been given the keys. But the keys did not fit the lock. They didn't open the door. Louis tried to force it, he tried going under and over it, he tried the back door and the front door, but nothing worked. They'd come all this way, Adèle had lied to her parents, and she was here — the only girl with four boys, joints, and alcohol — and the key wouldn't open the door.

"We can go through the garage," said Frédéric, who knew the house and was sure that it could be entered that way. "There's no car in there."

They had to smash the little window, which was six feet off the ground. Frédéric was the first one through. Louis gave Adèle a leg up and, not wanting to show any fear, she jumped down into the damp garage. They'd come all the way to the seaside just to find themselves locked in a dark garage, sitting on moldy towels spread out on the concrete floor. But they had alcohol, joints, even a guitar. In those hungry bellies, those puny chests, all of this good stuff should be enough to make up for the loss of the beach.

Adèle drank to give herself courage. The moment had come. She wouldn't try to get out of it. There were too few opportunities, too few secluded places, too few beach houses for Louis to back down now. And she'd already talked the talk. She'd told him that she knew about that kind of thing, that she wasn't afraid. That she'd seen other boys before. Sitting on the freezing floor, slightly drunk, she wondered if he would realize. If you could get away with that kind of lie or if it was always obvious.

The atmosphere darkened. There was a sort of gloom in the air. A childhood desire tightened her throat. One last jolt of innocence almost made her chicken out. The afternoon went faster than expected and the other boys found an excuse to leave the garage. She could hear them outside scratching around like rats. Louis undressed her. He lay on his back and sat her on top of him.

She hadn't imagined all this. This clumsiness, these labored gestures, these grotesque movements. The difficulty of making his penis go into her vagina. He didn't seem particularly happy, just furious, mechanical. He seemed as if he wanted to get somewhere but she didn't know where. He grabbed her hips and started thrusting back and forth. He told her she was crap at this, lumbering and inert. She said she thought she'd smoked too much pot. He put her on her side and that was even worse. He lay her in the fetal position and impatiently shoved himself inside her. She didn't know whether to move or let him take the lead, stay silent or make little moans.

They went home. In the bus, Louis sat next to her. He put his arm around her shoulders. So is this what it's like to be his woman? she wondered. She felt simultaneously dirty and proud, humiliated and victorious. She sneaked back into the house. Simone was watching television and Adèle rushed to the bathroom.

"You're taking a bath at this time of night?" her mother shrieked. "Who do you think you are, the Queen of Sheba?"

Adèle sank into the hot bath. She stuck a finger into her vagina in the hope of finding something. Some kind of proof. A sign. Her vagina was empty. She wished they'd had a bed, that there'd been more light in that little garage. She didn't even know if she'd bled.

Six euros ninety. Every day she gathers six euros ninety in loose change and buys a pregnancy test. It's become an obsession. Every morning when she wakes up she goes to the bathroom, takes the pink-and-white packet from the bottom of a toiletry bag where she's hidden it, and pees on the little strip. She waits five minutes. Five minutes of absolute anguish, and yet it's completely irrational. The test is negative. She is relieved for a few hours but that evening, after checking that her period still hasn't arrived, she goes back to the pharmacy and buys another test. This is perhaps what she fears most: becoming pregnant by another man. Not being able to explain it to Richard. Or, even worse, having to make love with her husband and then tell him that the child is his. And then she gets her period, to the sound of broken eggs. Her belly grows heavy and hard. She comes to savor the spasms that keep her in bed all evening, her knees pressed against her breasts.

There was a time when she used to take an AIDS test every week. As she waited for the result she would become paralyzed with anxiety. She would smoke joints when she woke up, starve herself all day, and end up roaming the paths around the Salpêtrière hospital, her hair disheveled, a coat over her pajamas, to pick up a yellow card with the word "negative" printed on it.

Adèle is afraid of dying. Her fear is intense: it grips her by the throat and stops all thought. So she starts palpating her belly, her breasts, the back of her neck, finding swellings that are, she feels sure, the signs of a fast-moving and horribly painful cancer. She vows to stop smoking. This resolution lasts an hour, an afternoon, a day. She throws away all her cigarettes, buys packets of chewing gum. She runs for hours around the rotunda in the Parc Monceau. Then she decides that it's not worth living while fighting against such a desperate desire, such an absolute need. That she would have to be insane or utterly stupid to inflict this deprivation on herself, to watch herself suffering and hope that it lasts as long as possible. She rummages through all her drawers, turns out her coat pockets, shakes out her handbags. And, when she's not lucky enough to find a forgotten packet somewhere, she goes out on to the little balcony and picks up a cigarette butt with a black filter, cuts the end off and sucks at it greedily.

Her obsessions devour her. She is helpless to stop them. Because her life requires so many lies, it has to be carefully organized — an exhausting activity that occupies her entire brain, that gnaws at her. Arranging a fake trip, inventing a pretext, renting a hotel room. Finding the right hotel. Calling the concierge ten times to check that the room has a bathtub, that it's not too noisy. Lying without trying too hard to justify herself. Justifications give rise to suspicions.

Choosing an outfit for a rendezvous, thinking about it constantly. Opening a cupboard in the middle of a meal and replying to Richard, when he asks her what she's up to: "Oh, sorry, I'm looking for a dress. I can't think where I've put it."

Checking her bank accounts, over and over. Withdrawing cash, and leaving no trace of it. Going into the red to buy lingerie, to pay for taxi trips and overpriced cocktails in hotel bars.

Being beautiful, being ready. Getting her

priorities mixed up, inevitably.

Missing a doctor's appointment for Lucien because of a kiss that went on too long. Being too ashamed to go back to that pediatrician, even though she was a good one. Being too lazy to choose a new one. Telling herself that, as his father is a doctor, Lucien doesn't really need a pediatrician at all.

She bought a flip phone. She never takes it out of her handbag and Richard knows nothing about it. She got a second computer, which she hides under the bed, on her side, near the window. She keeps no souvenirs, no receipts, no proof. She is wary of married men, sentimental men, hysterical men, old bachelors, young romantics, online lovers, friends of friends.

At four in the afternoon Richard calls her. He apologizes for being on duty again. That's two nights running and he should have warned her. But he felt obliged to accept; he owed this colleague a favor.

"Xavier? Remember him?"

"Oh yeah. The guy from the dinner party. Listen, I can't talk for long, I'm outside the school waiting for Lucien. I'll probably go to the cinema tonight, then. I'd already asked Maria to look after Lucien anyway."

"Okay, that's fine. You go and see the film, you can tell me all about it."

Thankfully he never does ask her to tell him all about it.

Tonight Adèle is seeing Xavier. The day they returned to Paris she locked herself in the bathroom to send him a text. "I'm back." They decided to meet tonight. Adèle bought herself a very plain white dress and a pair of polka-dotted tights. She'll wear flat shoes. Xavier is not very tall.

Outside the school, Adèle watches the mothers laugh together. They hold their children by the shoulders, promise to stop at the baker's and then at the merry-go-round. Lucien comes out dragging his coat along the ground.

"Put your coat on, Lucien. It's cold! Come here, I'll zip it up for you." Adèle crouches in front of her son, who pushes her and knocks her off balance.

"I don't want the coat!"

"Lucien, I'm not going to argue with you. Not now, in the street. Put your coat on." She slides her hand under her son's sweater and pinches the skin on his back very hard. She feels the soft flesh fold between her fingers. "Put it on, Lucien. No arguments."

Walking back home, the little boy's hand in hers, she feels guilty. Her stomach is in knots. Her son stops in front of every car they pass to talk about its shape and color, and she pulls on his arm, repeating: "Hurry up!" She tries to drag him forward but he resists, refuses to move an inch. Everyone is staring at them.

She wishes she were able to take her time. She wishes she could be patient, enjoy every moment with her son. But today she wants only one thing: to get rid of him as quickly as possible. It won't take long. In two hours she'll be free. He will have taken his bath, eaten dinner. They'll have fought, she'll have screamed. Maria will have arrived and Lucien will have started to cry.

She leaves the apartment. She stops outside a cinema, buys a ticket, and puts the stub in her coat pocket. She hails a taxi.

Adèle is sitting in the dark in an apartment building on Rue du Cardinal Lemoine. She is on a step midway between the first and second floors. She has not seen anyone. She is waiting.

He shouldn't be long now.

She is scared. Someone might enter, someone she doesn't know, someone who wants to hurt her. She forces herself not to look at her watch. She does not take her cell from her pocket. Nothing ever happens fast enough. She leans back, puts her handbag under her head, and lifts up her knee-length beige slip. It's a light slip — too light for the season — but it hovers through the air when you spin around, like a little girl's skirt. Adèle strokes her thigh with her fingernails. She slides her hand up slowly, pushes aside her panties, and puts her hand there. Firmly. She can feel her lips swelling, the blood rushing under the pulp of her fingertips. She closes her fist tight around her vulva. Scratches herself violently, from her anus to her clitoris. She turns her face to the wall, spreads her legs, and wets her fingers. Once, a man spat on her pussy. She liked that.

The index and middle fingers. That's all she needs. A hot, lively movement, like a dance. A regular caress, completely natural and utterly degrading. It's not working. She stops then tries again. She swings her head like a horse trying to shake the flies out of its nostrils. Only an animal can be good at such things. Maybe if she cries out, if she starts moaning, she'll find it easier to feel the spasm coming, the liberation, the pain, the anger. She whispers little *ah*s. But a moan shouldn't come from your mouth, it should come from deep in your belly. No, you'd have to be a beast to abandon yourself like that. You'd have to have no dignity, Adèle thinks, just as the building's front door opens. Someone has called the lift. She doesn't move. Shame he didn't take the stairs.

Xavier emerges from the lift and takes a key fob from his pocket. Adèle has taken off her shoes. As he opens the door, she puts her hands on his waist. He jumps and cries out.

"Oh, it's you! You scared me. That's a weird way to say hello, isn't it?"

She shrugs and walks into the bachelor apartment.

Xavier talks a lot. Adèle wishes he would hurry up and open the bottle of wine that he's been holding for the last fifteen minutes. Finally she gets up and hands him the corkscrew.

This is her favorite moment.

The moment before the first kiss, nudity, intimate caresses. That moment of anticipation when everything is still possible and when she is the mistress of the magic. She greedily drinks a mouthful of wine. A drop trickles over her lips and down her chin and drips on to the collar of her white dress before she can stop it. It's a detail of the story and she was the one who wrote it. Xavier is jittery and shy. He is not impatient; she is grateful to him for sitting at a distance from her, on that uncomfortable chair. Adèle is on the sofa, her legs folded beneath her. She stares at Xavier with her swamp eyes, viscous and impenetrable.

He moves his mouth toward her and an electric wave runs through her belly. It hits her pussy and explodes it, fleshy and moist, like a peeled fruit. The man's mouth tastes of wine and cigarillos. Of forests and the Russian countryside. She wants him, and this desire, to her, feels almost like a miracle. She wants it all: him, and his wife, and this affair, and these lies, and the texts they will send, and the secrets and the tears and even the inevitable good-bye. He slips her dress off. His surgeon's hands, long and bony, barely brush her skin. His gestures are assured, agile, delicious. He seems detached and then suddenly furious, uncontrollable. A strong sense of theater; Adèle is thrilled. He is so close now that her head starts to spin. She is breathing too hard to think. She is limp, empty, at his mercy.

He accompanies her to the taxi rank, presses his lips hard against her neck. Adèle dives into the cab, her flesh still drenched with love, hair tangled. Soaked with odors, caresses, and saliva, her skin has a new complexion. Every pore denounces her. Her gaze is liquid. She looks like a cat, nonchalant and mischievous. She tenses her vagina and a shiver runs through her whole body, as if the pleasure is not yet totally consumed, as if her body still harbors memories so vivid that she could, at any moment, summon them and make herself come.

Paris is orange and deserted. The icy wind

has swept the bridges, rid the city of pedestrians, cleansed the streets. Enveloped in a thick cape of fog, the city offers Adèle an ideal place for daydreaming. She feels almost like an intruder in this landscape, peering through the window like someone with her eye to a keyhole. The city appears infinite, she feels anonymous. It's hard to believe that she is connected with anyone, that anyone is waiting for her, expecting anything of her.

She goes home and pays Maria, who as always feels obliged to tell her: "He kept calling for you tonight. It took him a long time to fall asleep." Adèle gets undressed and sniffs her dirty clothes, which she rolls in a ball and hides in a cupboard. Tomorrow she will rub her nose in them, seek Xavier's smell.

She is in bed when the phone rings.

"Madame Robinson? You're the wife of Dr. Richard Robinson? Madame, I'm sorry for calling so late. Please don't panic, but your husband had a scooter accident about an hour ago on Boulevard Henri IV. He's conscious and his life is not in danger, but he has suffered serious trauma to his legs. He was brought here — to the Salpêtrière hospital — and we are conducting a series of tests. I can't tell you any more than that for now. You may come and see him whenever you like. I'm sure he would appreciate your support."

Adèle is sleepy. She doesn't really understand. She doesn't grasp the seriousness of the situation. She thinks vaguely that she could sleep for a bit, say that she didn't hear her phone ring. But no, it's too late. The night is ruined. She goes into Lucien's bedroom. "Lucien, darling, we have to go for a drive." She wraps him in a blanket and carries him in her arms. He doesn't wake up when she gets in the taxi. On the way there she calls Lauren several times, but is answered only by her polite voicemail message. Annoyed, increasingly frenetic, she keeps calling her over and over again.

Outside Lauren's apartment building, she asks the taxi to wait for her.

"I'm just going to drop my son here and then I'll come back."

In a strong Chinese accent, the driver demands some cash as security.

"Go fuck yourself," says Adèle, tossing him a twenty-euro note.

She enters the building, Lucien asleep on her shoulder, and rings Lauren's doorbell.

"Why didn't you answer me? Are you sulking?"

"Of course not," Lauren replies, mouth

dry and face creased. She is wearing a too-small kimono that barely covers her bottom. "I was asleep, that's all. What's happening?"

"I thought you were angry after the other night. I thought you didn't love me anymore, that you were sick of me, that you were keeping your distance . . ."

"What are you talking about? Adèle, what's going on?"

"Richard had a scooter accident."

"Oh shit."

"I don't think it's too serious. They'll have to operate on his leg, but he'll be okay. I have to go to the hospital, and I can't take Lucien. There's no one else I can ask."

"Yes, yes, of course, give him to me." Lauren holds out her arms. Adèle leans toward her and gently slides the boy's body into Lauren's chest. Lauren closes her arms around the blanket. "Keep me posted. And don't worry about him."

"I told you, I don't think it's serious."

"I was talking about your son," Lauren whispers as she closes the door.

Adèle calls a taxi. She is told she will have to wait ten minutes. She stands in the dark lobby, behind the large glass door. In safety. She is too frightened to wait in the street at

119

this time of night. She might be attacked, raped. She watches the taxi go past the building and park about two hundred yards farther on, at the corner of the street. "What a prick!" Adèle opens the door and runs toward the cab.

She sits in the waiting room on the sixth floor. "The doctor will come and see you as soon as he's finished." Adèle smiles shyly. She leafs through a magazine, her legs crossed until she starts to get pins and needles in her calves. She's been here for an hour now, watching the stretchers roll past, listening to the young doctors joking with the nurses. She has called Odile, who has decided to catch the first train tomorrow to come and see her son. "It must be hard for you, my dear Adèle. I'll take Lucien home with me, then you'll be able to look after Richard without worrying."

Adèle is not sad or upset. This accident, however, is a little bit her fault. If Xavier hadn't swapped shifts with Richard, if she hadn't suggested that ridiculous idea to him, if they hadn't been so desperate to see each other tonight, her husband would be home now, safe and sound. She would be sleeping peacefully beside him without having to face all the complications that this accident will undoubtedly cause.

But this accident is also perhaps a godsend. A sign, a release. For a few days at least she will have the house all to herself. Lucien will go to stay with his grandparents. No one will be able to monitor her comings and goings. At one point the thought crosses her mind that things could have turned out even better.

Richard could have died.

She would have been a widow.

A widow can be forgiven almost anything. Grief is a wonderful excuse. She could wallow in mistakes and conquests for the rest of her life, and everyone would say: "Her husband's death was too much for her. She never got over it." But no, that scenario does not hold water. Sitting in this waiting room, asked to fill out papers and questionnaires, she has to accept the fact that Richard is essential to her. She couldn't live without him. She would be completely defenseless, forced to confront the hideous reality of life. She would have to start again from scratch, do everything herself, waste time on paperwork that she could devote to love.

No, Richard must never die. Not before she does.

■ ■ ■ ■

"Mrs. Robinson? I'm Dr. Kovac."

Adèle carefully stands up. Her legs are so numb, she finds it hard to remain upright. "I was the one who talked to you earlier. I've just seen the scans and the injuries are serious. Thankfully the wounds on the right leg are superficial. But the left leg has multiple fractures, the tibial plateau has been shattered, and the ligaments are ruptured."

"All right. So what does that mean?"

"He'll go into surgery sometime in the next few hours. His leg will be in a cast, and we'll be looking at a long period of rehabilitation."

"How long will he stay here?"

"A week, maybe a little longer. Don't worry, your husband will soon be home with you again. We're prepping him for surgery now. I'll ask the nurse to call you when he's been taken back to his room."

"I'll wait here."

After an hour or so she moves to a different spot. She doesn't like sitting outside the elevator doors, which keep opening and revealing all the horrors of the world. She finds an empty chair at the end of the corridor, near the nurses' break room. She watches them going through files, preparing treatments, walking from room to room. She hears the shuffle of their slippers on the linoleum. She listens to their conversations. A nursing assistant pushes a trolley too hard and a glass falls to the floor. In room 6095 a female patient stubbornly refuses treatment. Adèle can't see her but she guesses that she is old and that the nurse is used to her tantrums. Then the voices fall silent. The corridor is plunged into darkness. Sickness gives way to sleep.

Three hours ago, Xavier's hand was on her cunt.

Adèle stands up. Her neck is very sore. She goes in search of the toilets, gets lost in the empty corridors, retraces her footsteps, goes around in circles. In the end she pushes open a plywood door and finds herself in a dilapidated bathroom. The bolt on the cubicle doesn't work. There's no hot water and she shivers as she splashes water on her face and hair. She rinses her mouth before confronting the coming day. In the corridor she hears someone speak her name. Yes, they really said Robinson. Are they looking for her? No, they're talking to her husband;

to Richard, lying on that stretcher. Richard, pale and sweating, looking frail and thin in his blue gown, is there, outside room 6090. His eyes are open, but Adèle finds it hard to believe that he's awake. His gaze is glassy. Only his hands, gripping tight to pull the sheet over his body, his hands, defending his modesty, only his hands prove that he is conscious.

The nurse pushes the stretcher into the room. She closes the door on Adèle, who waits for them to tell her she may enter. She doesn't know what to do with her arms. She is trying to think of something to say: a comforting phrase, a soothing word.

"You can go in now."

Adèle sits to the right of the bed. Richard barely turns his face toward her. He opens his mouth and thick threads of saliva stick to his lips. He smells bad. An odor of sweat and fear. She puts her head on the pillow and they fall asleep at the same time, forehead to forehead.

She leaves Richard at eleven. "I should go and pick up Lucien. Poor Lauren is waiting for me." In the lift she bumps into the surgeon who operated on her husband. He's wearing jeans and a leather jacket. He's young. Maybe still a junior doctor. She imagines him opening bodies, handling bones, sawing them, turning them over, taking them apart. She observes his hands, his long fingers which have spent the night bathed in blood and phlegm.

She lowers her eyes. She pretends not to recognize him. Once they are out in the street, though, she feels compelled to follow him. He walks quickly. She speeds up. She watches him from the opposite pavement. He takes a cigarette from his jacket. She crosses the road and stands in front of him.

"Have you got a light?"

"Oh, sure, hang on," he says, startled, patting the pockets of his jacket. "You're Dr.

Robinson's wife, aren't you? Don't worry. It's a bad fracture, but he's still young. He'll be back on his feet in no time."

"Yes, I know. You told me all that earlier when you came to the room. I'm not worried." He spins the wheel of his lighter. The flame flares and dies. He protects it with his right hand, but again a gust of wind blows it out. Adèle takes the lighter from him.

"Are you going home now?"

"Uh, yeah."

"Is someone expecting you?"

"Yeah. But . . . why? Can I help you?"

"Do you want to go for a drink?"

The doctor looks at her and bursts out laughing. A noisy, cheerful, childlike laugh. Adèle's face relaxes. She smiles, she is beautiful. This guy loves life. He has teeth like a white wizard's, a voluptuous gaze.

"Sure, why not? If you like."

Adèle visits Richard every day. Before she goes into his room she pokes her head through the doorway. If her husband is awake she gives him an embarrassed, sympathetic smile. She brings magazines, chocolates, a warm baguette, or some fruit. But he doesn't seem to like any of it. He lets the baguette go stale. The air is thick with the smell of overripe bananas.

He doesn't want to do anything. Not even chat with her as she sits on the uncomfortable blue stool to the right of the bed and desperately tries to make conversation. She leafs through magazines, commenting on the latest gossip, but Richard barely responds. In the end she falls silent. She looks out the window at this hospital the size of a town, the elevated railway and the Gare d'Austerlitz.

Richard has not shaved for a week and his

128

ragged black beard makes him look harsher. He has lost a lot of weight. His leg in a cast, he stares straight ahead at the wall, overwhelmed by the thought of all the long weeks ahead.

Each time, she convinces herself that she will spend the afternoon with him, keep him amused, wait for the doctor to do his rounds so she can ask questions. But no one comes. Time passes even more slowly because she has the feeling that they've been forgotten, as if no one is looking after them, as if this room does not exist and the afternoon stretches out endlessly before them. After half an hour she always ends up getting bored and leaving. She can't help feeling relieved as she exits his room.

She hates this hospital. These corridors where patients — in casts, bandaged, on crutches, with braces on their necks or backs — practice walking. These waiting rooms where people wait for the words that will change their lives. At night, in her sleep, she hears the cries of Richard's neighbor, a senile octogenarian with a broken thighbone who screams: "Leave me alone, I'm begging you, please just go away!"

One afternoon she is about to leave when a plump, chatty nurse enters the room. "Ah, that's good, your wife came to see you. She can help wash you. It'll be easier with two of us." Richard and Adèle look at each other, horribly embarrassed by the situation. Adèle rolls up the sleeves of her sweater and takes the washcloth that the nurse holds out to her.

"I'm going to lift him up and you can rub his back. Yes, that's it." Adèle moves the washcloth slowly over Richard's back, under his hairy armpits, across his shoulders. She goes down to his buttocks. She is as diligent and gentle as she can be. Richard lowers his head and she knows he is crying. "I can finish up on my own if that's okay with you," she says to the nurse, who is about to reply when she notices that Richard is sobbing softly. Adèle sits on the bed. She takes Richard's arm and rubs his skin, lingering over his long fingers. She doesn't know what to say. She has never had to look after her husband before and this role makes her sad and disconcerted. Whether broken or in good health, Richard's body is nothing to her. It provokes no emotion in her.

Thankfully she has Xavier.

"I can see that you're upset," Richard whispers suddenly. "I'm sorry I've been so withdrawn, so cold with you. I know this is all really hard for you too. But . . . I saw myself die, Adèle. I was so sleepy I couldn't

130

even keep my eyes open and then I lost control of my scooter. It all happened very slowly. I saw everything: the car coming toward me, the lamppost to my right. I skidded a long way. It seemed to last forever. I thought it was all over, that I was going to die because I'd worked too many hours. It opened my eyes. This morning I wrote an e-mail to the department head, resigning from my job. I'm leaving the hospital. I can't stand it here anymore. I've made an offer on the house and I expect to become a partner at the Lisieux clinic soon. You should hand in your notice at the newspaper. Don't wait till the last minute, it'd be a shame to leave them on bad terms. We're going to start a new chapter of our life, darling. Maybe, in the end, we won't look back on this accident in a purely negative light."

He looks up at her with his bloodshot eyes and smiles, and Adèle sees the old man with whom she will end her life. His sober face, his yellow complexion, his dry lips: this is her future. "I'm going to call the nurse. She can finish up without me. You should concentrate on getting better. Don't think about all this. Just get some rest. We'll talk about it again tomorrow." She wrings out the washcloth in a rage, drops it on the bedside table, and leaves the room with a wave of her hand.

It wakes her suddenly. She hardly has time to grasp the fact that she's naked and cold, that she fell asleep with her face in an overflowing ashtray. It makes her chest shudder, it twists her guts. She tries to close her eyes. She turns over and begs sleep to swallow her up, to rescue her from this ugly situation. With her eyelids shut she buries herself in the swaying bed. Her tongue spasms so hard she wants to scream with pain. Green flashes shoot through her head. Her pulse accelerates. The nausea flays her stomach. Her throat trembles and her stomach seems to empty, as if preparing for expulsion. She tries to lift her legs to get the blood back to her brain, but she's too weak. She just has time to crawl to the bathroom. She puts her head in the toilet bowl and starts throwing up a gray, acidic liquid. Violent retches wring out her entire body. She vomits from her mouth and her nose and she feels like she's dying. She thinks it has stopped and then it starts again. As she vomits for a second time, her body twists into a coil and then collapses, exhausted.

She doesn't move. Lying on the tile floor, she slowly catches her breath. The back of her neck is soaked with sweat. She starts to feel cold: a relief. She presses her knees against her chest and weeps softly. The tears deform her yellow face, cracking the dry veneer of makeup on her skin. She swings back and forth, disgusted and betrayed by her body. She rubs the tip of her tongue over her teeth and feels a bit of food stuck to her palate.

She doesn't know how much time has passed. She doesn't know whether she fell back asleep. She crawls over the tiles to the shower cubicle. Very carefully, step by step, she climbs to her feet. She is afraid she will faint, smash her skull on the bathtub, vomit yet again. Squatting, kneeling, on her feet. She can barely stand. She wants to sink her nails into the walls. She takes a deep breath and tries to walk in a straight line. Her nose is blocked, full of scabs. It hurts. Once she's in the shower she notices the blood trickling down her thighs. She doesn't dare look at her crotch but she knows it is raw, torn and swollen like the face of someone who's been beaten up.

She doesn't remember much. Her body is her only clue. She didn't want to spend the evening alone, she remembers that. It was agonizing, the thought of all those empty hours, not knowing how she would fill them, alone in her apartment. Within an hour Mehdi replied to the message she left on his website. He arrived at nine — with a friend and five grams of cocaine, as agreed. Adèle had made herself beautiful: just because you're paying for it doesn't mean you shouldn't make an effort. They sat in the living room. She liked Mehdi straight-away. His shaved head, his young thug's face, his brown gums and sharp teeth. He was wearing a chain on his wrist. His nails were bitten to the quick. He was admirably vulgar. The friend was blond and quiet. A young, skinny boy named Antoine, who took an hour to remove his jacket.

They looked a bit surprised by the apart-ment, with its modern, sophisticated decor. Sitting on the sofa, they were like two little boys embarrassed to be having tea with a grown-up. Adèle opened a bottle of cham-pagne and Mehdi asked her what she did for a living.

"I'm a journalist."

"A journalist? Fuck me, that's wicked!"

He took the sachet from his pocket and waved it in front of Adèle's face. "Oh yeah, hang on!" She turned around and took a DVD cover from the bookshelf: one of Lucien's cartoon shows. Mehdi laughed and poured out six lines on the smooth plastic. "After you. This is good stuff, you know," he kept repeating. And he was right.

Adèle could hardly feel her teeth anymore. Her nostrils stung and she felt a joyful, compulsive desire for alcohol. She grabbed the champagne bottle and threw her head back. When the liquid started dripping down her cheeks, into the hollows of her neck, soaking her clothes, she figured it was time. Antoine crouched behind her. He started unbuttoning Adèle's blouse. They knew exactly what they were doing; it was like a perfectly choreographed ballet. Mehdi licked her breasts and put his hand between her thighs while Antoine grabbed her by the hair.

Adèle lets herself slide down the wall. She crouches under the jet of hot water. She needs to pee but her groin is hard, as if the muscle has hardened to bone during the night. She curls her toes, clenches her jaw,

136

and when, at last, the rank urine starts trickling down her thigh, she groans with pain. Her vagina is just a shard of broken glass now, a maze of ridges and fissures. A thin layer of ice with frozen corpses floating beneath it. Her mons pubis, which she shaves every day, is purple.

She was the one who asked for it. She can't blame them. She asked Mehdi to do it, after an hour of screwing, an hour of him inside her, of Antoine inside her, of games and swaps. She couldn't hold back any longer. She told him: "It's not enough." She wanted to feel it. She thought she could take it. Five times, maybe ten, he lifted up his leg and his sharp, bony knee smashed into her vulva. To start with, he was careful. He exchanged a surprised, slightly mocking look with Antoine. He shrugged and lifted his leg. He didn't understand. But then, seeing her writhe, hearing her cries that were no longer human, he got a taste for it.

Afterward . . . afterward, nothing else was possible. Afterward, she may have fainted. Perhaps they talked a bit longer. In any case, she woke up here, naked in an empty apartment. She hobbles slowly out of the shower, clinging tight to the wall, to the countertop. She grabs a towel and wraps it around her, then sits carefully, very carefully, on the edge of the bed. She looks at herself in the full-length mirror. She is old and deathly pale. The slightest movement sickens her. Even thinking is enough to make the walls spin.

She should eat something. Drink something cold and sweet. She knows that the first mouthful will be delicious, it will quench her thirst, but once the liquid hits her empty stomach she will feel intensely nauseated, she will have a terrible migraine. She'll have to resist. Lie down again. Drink a little bit, sleep a lot.

The fridge is empty anyway. Adèle has not been shopping since Richard was hospitalized. The apartment is filthy. In the bedroom, clothes are strewn all over the place, pairs of panties litter the floor. A dress lies sleeping on the arm of the living-room sofa. Unopened letters are piled up in the kitchen. In the end, she will lose them all or throw them away. She'll tell Richard that there wasn't any mail. Adèle has not been to work all week. She promised Cyril an article that she is incapable of writing. She has been ignoring his texts and calls. Finally, in the middle of the night, she sends him a pathetic message explaining that she is spending her days at the hospital looking after her husband. That she'll be back on Monday.

She sleeps fully dressed, she eats in her bed. She is cold all the time. Her bedside table is covered with half-eaten containers of yogurt, spoons, and bits of dried bread. She sees Xavier whenever he has time, in the apartment on Rue du Cardinal Lemoine. When he calls, she gets out of bed, takes a long hot shower, throws her clothes on the floor, and empties her cupboard. Her bank account is overdrawn but she takes a taxi anyway. Every day she needs a little more makeup to camouflage the bags under her eyes, to brighten up her dull complexion.

Her telephone rings. She pats the duvet, slowly lifts up the pillows. She can hear it but she can't find it. Then she lifts her foot and sees it. She looks at the screen. Six missed calls. All from Richard, minutes apart. Six frenzied calls. Six furious calls.

Today is January 15.

The day Richard gets out. He is waiting for her. It's January 15 and she'd forgotten. She gets dressed: a pair of old jeans and a man's cashmere sweater.

She sits down.

She does her hair and makeup.

Sits down.

She tidies the living room, rolls her clothes up in a ball, then leans back against the kitchen cupboards, her forehead glazed with sweat. She looks for her handbag. It's on the floor, completely empty.

She has to go and pick up Richard.

In the summer, Adèle's parents would rent a small apartment near Le Touquet. Kader would spend all day at the bar with a gang of holiday friends. Simone would play bridge and sunbathe on the terrace, a reflective disk around her neck.

Adèle enjoyed being left alone in the apartment. She would smoke mint cigarettes on the balcony. She would dance in the middle of the living room and rummage through the drawers. One afternoon she found a copy of *The Unbearable Lightness of Being* that must have belonged to the apartment's owners. Her parents didn't read that kind of book. Her parents didn't read any kinds of book, in fact. She flicked through the pages randomly and came upon a scene that moved her to tears. The words seemed to resonate deep within her. Each sentence shot an electric current through her body. She clenched her jaw, tensed the muscles of her vagina. For the first time in her life, she felt the desire to touch herself. She pulled her panties up so tight that the fabric burned her flesh.

"She was nearly immobile while he undressed her. When he kissed her, her lips failed to react. But suddenly she felt her groin becoming moist, and she was afraid."

She put the book back in its place, in the little chest of drawers in the living room, and at night she thought about it. She tried to remember the exact words, to rediscover their music, and then she couldn't hold out any longer. She got out of bed and opened the drawer. She looked at the yellow book jacket and felt new sensations awakening beneath her light gown. She hardly dared pick it up. She hadn't marked the page, had left no trace of her presence in the middle of that story. But each time she ended up finding the chapter that had stirred her so deeply.

"The excitement she felt was all the greater because she was excited against her will. In other words, her soul did condone the proceedings, albeit covertly. But she also knew that if the feeling of excitement was to continue, her soul's approval would have to keep mute. The moment it said its yes aloud, the moment it tried to take an active part in the love scene, the excitement would subside. For what made the soul so excited was that the body was acting against its will; the body was betraying it, and the soul was looking on.

Then he pulled off her panties and she was completely naked."

She repeated those phrases like a mantra. She rolled them around her tongue. Wallpapered the back of her mind with them. Very quickly, she understood that desire was unimportant. She didn't want men she would have to approach. It wasn't for the flesh she yearned, but for the situation. Being taken. Observing the look on a man's face when he came. Filling herself up. Tasting another's saliva. Miming epileptic orgasms, lascivious pleasure, animal satisfaction. Watching a man leave, traces of blood and semen under her fingernails.

Eroticism covered everything. It masked the banality and vanity of things. It gave a new depth to her adolescent afternoons, to birthday parties and even family reunions, where there was always an old uncle to ogle her breasts. This quest abolished all rules, all codes. Friendships, ambitions, schedules . . . it made them all impossible.

Adèle is neither proud nor ashamed of her conquests. She keeps no records, recollects no names, no situations. She forgets everything very quickly, and that is a good thing. How could she remember so many different skins and smells? How could she recall the memory of the weight of each body on hers, the width of their hips, the size of their penis? She has no clear memories of them, and yet these men are the sole landmarks of her existence. Each season, each birthday, each event in her life corresponds to a lover with a blurred face. In the depths of her amnesia there exists the reassuring sensation of having existed a thousand times through the desires of others. And when, years later, she happens to bump into a man who tells her in a deep and slightly shaky voice: "It took me quite a while to get over you," she draws an immense satisfaction from this. As if all of it has not been in vain. As if, in spite of her best intentions, some sort of meaning is somehow mixed up in this eternal repetition.

Some of them remained close to her, touched her more than others. Adam, for example, whom she likes to think of as a friend. Even though she met him on a dating website, she feels close to him. Sometimes she drops by at Rue Bleue, keeps her clothes on, and smokes a joint with him, in the bed that serves him as office and living room. She puts her head on his arm and she enjoys this easy camaraderie. He has never made any comments or asked any questions about her life. He is not intelligent or profound, and she likes that.

Some of them she grows attached to; she finds it hard to let them go. Now that she thinks about it, this attachment seems hazy; she no longer understands anything about it. At the time, though, nothing else seems to matter. That was true for Vincent and, before him, for Olivier, whom she met during a reporting trip to South Africa. She waited to hear from them with the same intensity she waits now for Xavier's messages. She wanted them to burn for her, wanted them to love her to the point of losing everything, even though she has never lost anything.

She could exit the stage now. Take a rest. Leave it up to fate and settle for Richard. It would probably be a good idea to stop now, before everything falls apart, before she is too old or too weak. Before becoming pitiful, before losing her magic and her dignity.

It's true that it's a very nice house.

Especially the little terrace, where she should plant a lime tree and install an old bench that they would let gently rot and become mossy. Far from Paris, in that small provincial house, she would give up the very thing that she thinks defines her, her true self. The very thing that, since no one else knows about it, represents her greatest act of defiance. If she abandoned that part of herself, she would become merely what everyone else sees. A surface without depth, without a flipside. A body without shadow. She would no longer be able to tell herself: "Let them think whatever they want. They'll never know the truth."

In that pretty house, in the shade of the lime tree, she would no longer be able to escape. Day after day, she would bump into herself. While shopping for food, doing laundry, helping Lucien with his homework, she would have to find a reason to live. Something beyond the prosaic realities which, even as a child, suffocated her, made her think of family life as a dreadful punishment. How she wanted to vomit up those endless days of being together, cherishing one another, watching the little ones sleep, arguing at bathtime, looking for things to do. Men rescued her from her childhood. They dragged her from the mud of adolescence and she traded childish passivity for the lasciviousness of a geisha.

"If you drove a car, you could have picked up your husband yourself. You'd be more independent, at least, don't you think?" Lauren is annoyed. In the car Adèle tells her about her night. She doesn't tell her everything. She hesitates, then finally admits that she needs to borrow some money. "I knew that Richard kept money in the house. But I wasn't supposed to spend it, you see? I'll get it back to you very soon, I promise." Lauren sighs and nervously taps the steering wheel. "All right, all right, I'll give it to you."

Richard is waiting for them in his room, with his bag in his lap. He is impatient. Lauren takes care of the administrative details while Adèle follows her, silent and tired, through the hospital corridors. She holds the ticket with their number on it while they wait in the admissions office. When their number is called, she says: "That's us." But it's Lauren who actually speaks to the blond woman behind the desk.

As soon as they enter the apartment, Adèle shrinks into herself. She could have put a vase of flowers on the little writing desk. She could have loaded the dishwasher. Bought some wine or beer. A bar of that chocolate that Richard loves. She could have hung up the coats that are sprawled over the chairs in the living room, washed the bathroom sink. Shown that she cares. Prepared a surprise. Been ready.

"All right, I'll get us something for lunch," Lauren says.

"I didn't have time to go shopping," Adèle explains. "I'm sorry, I wasn't very organized. I'll go and buy some food while you take a nap. Anything you want. Just tell me, okay?"

"It doesn't matter. I'm not hungry anyway."

Adèle helps Richard on to the sofa. She gently lifts the leg inside the plaster cast then puts it down on top of a cushion. She arranges the crutches on the floor.

Days pass and Richard does not move.

Life goes on. Lucien returns. Adèle goes back to work. She wishes she could lose herself in work, but she feels sidelined. Cyril greets her coldly. "You know Ben Ali was deposed while you were playing doctors and nurses? I left you messages, I don't know if you got them, but in the end we sent Bertrand."

She feels even more distanced from her colleagues by the atmosphere of sentimentality that pervades the office. For days on end, they seem to do nothing but watch images from Tunisia on the television screen in the middle of the office. A crowd of young people on Avenue Bourguiba noisily celebrating victory. Women weeping in the arms of soldiers.

Adèle looks at the screen. She recognizes everything. The avenue where she has walked so many times. The entrance of the Carlton Hotel, where she smoked cigarettes on the top-floor balcony. The tram, the taxis, the cafés where she would pick up men who smelled of tobacco and milky coffee. Back then all she could do as a journalist was listen to the melancholy of a people, take the lifeless pulse of Ben Ali's country. Her articles were always sad, dull, resigned.

Dumbstruck, her colleagues stand there, hands over mouths. They hold their breath. Now the images show Tahrir Square in flames. A chanting crowd. Effigies burning. Poems spoken into microphones. Talk of revolution. On February 11, at 5:03 p.m., Vice President Suleiman announces the resignation of Hosni Mubarak. The journalists yell and leap into one another's arms. Laurent turns to Adèle. He's in tears.

"Amazing, isn't it? And to think you could have been there. God, you were so unlucky — your husband having that accident."

Adèle shrugs. She gets up and puts on her coat.

"Aren't you staying? We're all going to follow it here live. Something like this only happens once in a career!"

"No, I'm going. I have to get home."

Richard needs her. He called three times this afternoon. "Don't forget my medicine." "Will you remember to buy trash bags?" "When are you getting home?" He is waiting for her. He can't do anything without her.

In the morning Adèle undresses him. She slides his boxer shorts down over the plaster cast while he stares up at the ceiling, muttering a prayer or an insult, depending on how he feels. She covers the cast with a trash bag that smells of paraffin, tapes it to his thigh, and helps Richard into the shower. He sits on a plastic chair and she lifts his leg on to the stool that she bought for him at Monoprix. After ten minutes he shouts, "I'm done!" and she hands him a towel. She accompanies him to the bed, where he lies down, out of breath. She tears off the tape, removes the plastic bag, and helps him to put on clean boxer shorts, trousers, socks. Before heading off to work she leaves a bottle of water on the coffee table, along with some bread, a handful of painkillers, and the telephone.

During the week she is so tired that she sometimes falls asleep at ten o'clock, fully dressed. She pretends not to see the cardboard boxes piling up in the entrance hall. She acts as if nothing is about to happen. As if she can't hear her husband asking her: "Have you talked to Cyril yet? Don't forget you have to hand in your notice."

On weekends the three of them are alone in the apartment. Adèle suggests they invite some friends over to take their minds off things. Richard has no desire to socialize with anyone. "I don't want them to see me in this state." Richard is irascible, aggressive. Normally so composed, he frequently works himself into a rage. She thinks that perhaps the accident shook him up more than she realized.

One Sunday she takes Lucien to the park on the hill of Montmartre. They sit on the edge of a frozen sandpit. Their hands are cold. Lucien has fun smashing the sandcastles conscientiously constructed by a blond child. The child's mother, cell phone stuck to her ear, walks over to Lucien and, without ending her phone conversation, pushes him backward. "What the hell do you think you're doing, you little brat? Leave my son alone. And don't touch his toys."

Lucien runs into his mother's arms, staring at the little blond kid who is crying, his nose smeared with snot.

"Come on, Lucien. Let's go home."

Adèle gets to her feet and picks up her son, who starts crying and refuses to leave. She walks along the sandpit and, with her boot heel, crushes the blond boy's sandcastle, then kicks his plastic buckets to the other end of the park. She does not turn around when the mother yells hysterically: "Hey, you!"

"Let's go home, Lucien. It's too cold."

When she opens the door, the apartment is silent. Richard has fallen asleep on the living-room sofa and Adèle slowly undresses her son, a finger to her lips. She puts him to bed and leaves a note on the coffee table. "Gone shopping."

Boulevard de Clichy. Outside the window of a sex shop an old man in a dirty raincoat points to a red vinyl maid's outfit. The black saleswoman with enormous breasts nods and invites him inside. Adèle passes tourists laughing outside erotic displays. She observes an old German couple who are choosing a DVD.

Outside a peep show a fat blond woman parades in the rain.

"A little dance. You won't be disappointed!"

"But you can see perfectly well that I'm taking my son for a walk," responds a man in his thirties, outraged.

"No problem. You can leave the stroller outside. I'll look after it for you."

On the median strip shady-looking men drink big cans of beer or cheap bottles of

155

vodka while they wait to be given a job to do. She can hear voices speaking Arabic, Serbian, Wolof, Chinese. Couples take their children for walks amid groups of drunks and smile when they see police patrols on bicycles.

Adèle enters the long corridor with the pink velvet carpet, its walls covered with photographs of women's bodies entwined, tongues out, buttocks spread. She greets the security guard. He knows her. He's sold her cannabis on several occasions and she gave him Richard's number when his sister was diagnosed with stomach cancer. Since then he's let her in without paying. He knows that all she ever does is watch anyway.

On Saturday evenings the place is sometimes sold out with boys here to lose their virginity or drunk office workers celebrating a new account. This afternoon there are only three clients sitting in front of the seedy little stage. A very thin middle-aged black man. A guy in his fifties, probably from out of town, who keeps checking his watch to make sure he's not going to miss his train. And, at the back of the room, an Arab who gives Adèle a disgusted look as she enters.

Adèle goes up to the black man. She leans over him. He turns to look at her, the whites of his eyes yellow and glassy, and smiles

156

shyly. His teeth are rotten. She remains standing, her eyes riveted to his calloused hands, his open fly, his moistened, veiny hard-on.

She hears the man behind her grumble and sigh.

"Hchouma."

"What did you say?"

The old Arab does not lift his head. He continues to stare sideways at the woman on the stage, who licks her fingers and then moans as she puts them on her tits.

"Hchouma."

"I can hear you, you know. I understand what you're saying."

He does not react.

The black man grabs Adèle by the arm and tries to calm her down.

"Let me go!"

The old Arab stands up. Malice in his eyes. His jowls darkened by a three-day beard. He stares at her for a long time. Observes her expensive shoes, her man's jacket, her clear skin. Her wedding ring.

He spits on the ground and leaves.

Out in the street Adèle is in a daze. Shaking with rage. Night has already fallen. She stuffs earbuds into her ears. She goes into a supermarket, wanders from aisle to aisle, carrying her empty basket. Even the idea of eating disgusts her. She picks up food at random, waits in line. She does not remove her earbuds. When it's her time to pay she turns the volume up. She looks at the young cashier, fingerless gloves on her hands, the varnish on her nails peeling. If the cashier talks to her, Adèle is going to cry. But the woman says nothing. She is used to clients who don't greet her.

The mechanism has jammed. A terrible anxiety nests within her. She is dreadfully thin, the skin literally stretched over her bones. In her eyes the streets seem haunted by an army of lovers. She keeps getting lost. She forgets to look both ways before crossing the road and is startled by the sound of car horns. One morning she thought she saw an ex-lover as she was coming out of her apartment. Her heart stopped and she took Lucien in her arms to hide her face. She started walking fast, in the wrong direction. She kept turning around, certain that she was being followed.

At home she fears the sound of the doorbell, listens out for footsteps in the stairwell. She checks the post. It took her a week to cancel the contract for the white phone, which she never found. She struggles to resign herself to it. She is surprised by sentimental feelings. Already she imagines them blackmailing her, spreading her secrets, going into the most sordid details. Slow and cumbersome, Richard is an easy beast to hunt. They will find him, they will tell him. Every time she leaves the apartment her stomach is in knots. She retraces her footsteps, fearful that she's forgotten something, that she's left behind compromising evidence.

"Are you all right? Do you need anything?"

She has put her husband and her son in pajamas. She's fed them. She rushes outside, feeling that she's done her duty and needing to be taken. She doesn't know why Xavier is so determined to eat at a restaurant. She would rather have gone to Rue du Cardinal Lemoine, stripped down as soon as she got through the door, exhausted herself. Not spoken a word.

"Thai or Russian?"

"Russian," replies Adèle. "We can drink vodka."

Xavier has not made a reservation but he knows the owner of this restaurant in the eighth arrondissement, a lair of businessmen and prostitutes, film stars and chic journalists. They are seated at a small table next to the window and Xavier orders a bottle of vodka. This is the first time they

160

have eaten dinner together. Adèle has always avoided eating in front of him. With him.

She doesn't look at the menu. She lets him choose for her. "I trust you." She barely touches her crayfish salad, preferring to freeze her fingers on the block of ice around the vodka bottle. Her throat burns and the alcohol sloshes around her empty stomach.

"Allow me to serve you, madame."

The waiter, contrite, comes over to their table.

"You may as well sit down with us, then."

Adèle laughs and Xavier looks away. She is embarrassing him.

They do not have much to say to each other. Adèle bites the insides of her cheeks and tries to find a topic of conversation. For the first time, Xavier talks about Sophie. He pronounces her name and his children's names. He says he feels ashamed, that he doesn't know where all this is leading. That he is finding it harder and harder to keep lying. Finding excuses is exhausting, he says.

"Why are you talking about her?"

"Would you rather I thought about her and didn't say anything?"

Xavier disgusts her. He bores her. This affair is already dead. It is now nothing more than a frayed scrap of paper on which they continue drawing like children. It's worn out.

She is wearing skintight gray jeans and a pair of high heels that she has never worn before. Her blouse is too low-cut. She is vulgar. When they leave the restaurant, Adèle finds it difficult to walk. Her legs bend like a newborn giraffe's. Her soles are slippery and the vodka is making her heels sway. Even though she is clinging tight to Xavier's arm, she stumbles over a curb and falls to the ground. A passerby rushes over to help her up. Xavier waves the man away. He can deal with this.

She is in pain and vaguely ashamed but she laughs, like a fountain spurting jets of icy water. She leads Xavier into the lobby of an apartment building. She doesn't hear him when he says: "No, stop it, you're crazy." She pushes herself against him, covers his face with wet, desperate kisses. She puts a hand on his crotch and he tries to push it away. He tries to stop her pulling his trousers down but she is already on her knees and, eyes wild, he is caught halfway between pleasure and the fear that someone might enter the lobby. She stands up, leans against the wall, and wriggles her too-tight jeans down her thighs. He penetrates her, sliding inside her liquid, generous body. She looks up at him with moist eyes and, miming modesty, aping emotion, she says: "I love you. I love you, you know." She holds his face and, under her fingertips, she can feel him surrender. She is stronger than his scruples. Like a rat numbed by the sound of her flute, he will follow her to the end of the world.

"We could make another life together," she whispers. "Take me with you."

He puts his clothes back on. Eyes like velvet, cheeks cool.

"See you on Friday, my love."

On Friday she will tell him that it's all over. With him, with everyone. She will find some dramatic excuse, something bigger than either of them. She will say that she is pregnant, that she is dying, that Richard has found out.

She will tell him that she is starting a new life.

"Hello, Richard."

"Sophie? Hello."

Xavier's wife stands in the doorway. She is elegantly dressed and made-up. Her fingers cling nervously to the strap of her handbag.

"I should have called first but I would have had to explain why I needed to see you, and I didn't want to do that to you by telephone. I can come back later if you want, I . . ."

"No, no, come in, sit down."

Sophie enters the apartment. She helps Richard with his plaster cast. She leans the crutches against the wall and sits facing him, in the blue chair.

"It's about Xavier."

"Yes?"

"And Adèle."

"Adèle."

"Last night we had friends over for dinner. They were late and I wanted to check my messages, to see if there was a problem." She swallows her saliva. "I have the same type of phone as Xavier. He'd left his on the table, in the entrance hall, and I picked it up. It was a mistake, I promise, I didn't mean to do it. I could never have . . . Anyway, I read it. A message from a woman. Very graphic. At the time I didn't say anything. Our guests arrived, we ate dinner. We had a nice evening, in fact, I don't think anyone suspected a thing. When they left I confronted Xavier. He spent ten minutes denying it. He claimed it was a patient who was harassing him, some madwoman, he said he didn't even know her name. And then he confessed everything. I think he was relieved. After a while I couldn't get him to stop. He says that he can't help himself, that it's beyond his control. He says he's in love with her."

"In love with Adèle?" Richard lets out a sardonic laugh.

"You don't believe me? Do you want to see the message? I have it with me . . ."

Richard leans slowly toward the phone that Sophie holds out to him and deciphers the message like a child, syllable by syllable. "I have to escape. I'm suffocating without you. I can't wait for Wednesday!"

"They had plans to meet on Wednesday. He was the one who mentioned Adèle. He told me it was her. If you could only hear him talk about her, it's . . ."

Sophie starts to sob. Richard wishes she would leave. Now. She is preventing him from thinking. She is preventing him from feeling the pain.

"Does he know you're here?"

"Oh no, I didn't say anything to him. He would go crazy. I don't even know what I'm doing here. I almost turned back when I got to your door. It's so ridiculous, so humiliating."

"Don't tell him. Whatever you do, don't tell him anything. Please."

"But . . ."

"Tell him he has to deal with this, put an end to it. Whatever happens, Adèle mustn't know that I know."

"All right."

"Promise me."

"I promise, Richard. Yes, I promise."

"And now, you have to go."

"Of course, I'm sorry. But Richard, what are we going to do? What will become of us?"

"Us? Nothing will become of us. We'll never see each other again, Sophie."

He opens the door.

"You know, it's Xavier you should feel sorry for. Forgive him. Or . . . Well, do what you want. It's none of my business."

For a child, flip phones are a source of great amusement. They light up when you open them. You can snap them shut and trap your fingers. It was Lucien who found the white phone. Adèle had gone out to buy a stool so that Richard could use the shower. She called from Castorama. "They don't have any here. I'm going to try Monoprix." Lucien was in the living room, playing with the flip phone.

"Who does that phone belong to, sweetie? Where did you find it? Where was it?"

"Where?" the child repeats.

Richard takes the phone from his son.

"Hello? Hello? Is Mommy there?"

Lucien laughs.

Richard looks at the phone. An old model. Someone could have forgotten it here. A friend who dropped by. Lauren, perhaps, or maybe even Maria, the babysitter. He opens it. The wallpaper is a photograph of Lucien.

In the photo he is a baby, asleep on the sofa, his little body covered by one of Adèle's cardigans. Richard is about to close it.

He has never gone through his wife's things. Adèle once told him how, when she was a teenager, Simone used to open her mail and read the letters her lovers sent her. While she was at school her mother would rummage through her desk drawers; one time she looked under the mattress and found the ridiculous private journal that Adèle kept. She used a knife to open the padlock and then she read out the contents that evening over dinner. She was laughing so hard she could barely breathe. Fat, mocking tears rolled down her cheeks. "Isn't that hilarious? Kader, come on, it's hilarious, isn't it?" Kader said nothing. But he didn't laugh.

For Richard that episode was a partial explanation of Adèle's character. Her obsession with locks, with tidying everything away. Her paranoia. He told himself that that was why she slept with her handbag on her side of the bed, with her little black notebook under her pillow.

He looks at the phone. In front of the picture of Lucien a yellow envelope is flashing, with the words "Unread message." Richard lifts his arm out of reach of Lucien, who is trying to grab the toy. "I want the phone!" Lucien squeals. "I want hello!"

Richard reads the message. That one and the others that follow it. He clicks on the contacts list. Scrolls through the staggering number of men's names.

Adèle should be home soon. That is all he thinks. She will come back and he doesn't want her to know that he knows.

"Lucien, where did you find the phone?"

"Where?"

"Yes, Lucien, where. Where did you find it?"

"Where?" the child repeats.

Richard holds him by the shoulders and shakes him, shouting: "Where was it? Where was the phone? Where?"

The boy stares at his father. His mouth twists and, head down, he points with his chubby little finger at the sofa.

"There. Under."

"Under the sofa?"

Lucien nods. Using his hands to support himself, Richard maneuvers himself to the floor. The plaster cast bangs against the wooden floorboards. He lies flat, turns his head to the side, and sees, beneath the sofa, several envelopes, a pink leather glove, and a familiar orange box.

The brooch.

He grabs his crutches and uses one to slide the orange box toward him. He is sweating. His leg hurts.

"Lucien, come here, we're going to play. You can see Daddy's on the floor, right, so let's play with your trucks. You want to? You want to play with me?"

He sleeps beside her. He watches her eat. He listens to the sound of the water when she takes a shower. He calls her at the office. He makes remarks about her clothes, her scent. Every night he asks her, in a deliberately annoying voice: "You're home very late. Where have you been? Who did you see? What were you doing?" He refuses to wait for the weekend to pack their stuff into cardboard boxes, knowing perfectly well that this drives her mad. Let her worry, let her fear, day after day, that he might, despite all her precautions, find something: a document, a mistake, some kind of proof. He has signed the sale agreement and Adèle has initialed the pages. He has hired movers and paid the deposit. He has enrolled Lucien in the local school.

He says nothing about his discovery.
He goes into the bedroom when she's get-

ting dressed and notices the scratches at the base of her neck. The thumb-shaped bruise just below her elbow. He stands in the doorway, face pale, hand tensed around his crutch. He watches as she covers herself with a big gray towel to put on her panties, like a little girl.

At night, lying next to her, he thinks about compromises. Arrangements. About his parents' arrangement, which no one talked about but everyone knew about. He thinks about Henri, his father, who used to rent a small apartment in town where, every Friday afternoon, he would meet a thirty-year-old woman. Odile discovered this. They argued about it in the kitchen. A frank, almost moving argument. Richard, an adolescent at the time, could hear scraps of their conversation from his bedroom. They came to an agreement, for the good of the children, for the sake of appearances. Henri ultimately gave up his bachelor pad and Odile, triumphant and dignified, welcomed him back into the bosom of the family.

Richard says nothing. He has no one in whom he can confide. He can't stand the idea of anyone looking at him as a pathetic cuckold, the poor naive husband. He has no desire to hear anyone's advice. Above all, he does not want anyone's pity.

Adèle has ripped up his world. She has sawn the legs off the furniture, she has scratched all the mirrors. She has spoiled the taste of everything. Memories, promises . . . none of it means anything any more. Their life is a fake. For himself, even more than for her, he feels a profound disgust. He looks at everything now through new eyes, and what he sees is dirty and sad. If he says nothing, perhaps it will hold firm anyway. What do they matter, really, those foundations that he worked so hard to lay? What does the solidity of a life matter, or honesty, or transparency? Perhaps if he keeps quiet, it will somehow not collapse. Probably all he has to do is close his eyes. And sleep.

But Wednesday arrives and he is restless, anxious. At five in the afternoon he receives a text from Adèle. She says they're behind schedule and it looks like she's going to have to work late. Without thinking, he writes: "You have to come home. I'm in a lot of pain. I need you." She doesn't reply.

At seven she arrives at the apartment. She avoids looking at Richard with her blood-shot eyes and asks him irritably: "What's going on? Is the pain really that bad?"

"Yes."

"But you've taken your pills, haven't you? What else can I do?"

"Nothing. Nothing at all. I just wanted you here. I didn't want to be alone."

He opens his arms and gestures for her to sit next to him on the sofa. She approaches, rigid and cold, and he holds her tight. He could strangle her. He can feel her tremble in his arms, can sense her staring into space, and he presses her close to him, seething with hate. Both he and she, in each other's arms, wish they were elsewhere. Their repulsion merges, and this false tenderness turns to outright loathing. She tries to free herself and he tightens his grip on her. Into her ear, he says:

"You never wear your brooch, Adèle."

"My brooch?"

"The one I gave you. You've never worn it."

"There really hasn't been an occasion to wear it, since the accident."

"Put it on, Adèle. I would like that."

"I'll put it on next time we go out, I promise. Maybe even tomorrow when I go to work, if you want. Let me get up, Richard. I'm going to make dinner."

"No, stay here," he orders. "Sit with me."

He grabs her arm and squeezes it.

"You're hurting me."

"Don't you like that?"

"What's wrong with you?"

"Doesn't Xavier do that to you? Don't you play these little games?"

"What are you talking about?"

"Oh, stop. You disgust me. If I wanted to, I could kill you, Adèle. I could strangle you right now."

"Richard."

"Shut up. Just shut your mouth. Your voice sickens me. Your smell sickens me. You're an animal, a monster. I know everything. I read all those vile messages. I found the e-mails, I put it all together. My head is filled with it now. I don't have a single memory that isn't mixed up with one of your lies."

"Richard."

"Stop it! Stop saying my name like an idiot!" he screams. "Why, Adèle? Why? You have no respect for me, for our life, for our son . . ." Richard starts to sob. He covers his eyes with his trembling hands. Adèle stands up. She is petrified by the sight of his tears.

"I don't know if you can understand, if you can believe me. But it's nothing against you, Richard. It never was, I promise. I just can't help myself. It's beyond my control."

"Beyond your control. What a load of crap. Who knows about this?"

"No one, I promise."

"Stop lying! Don't you think you've done enough damage already? No lies."

"Lauren," she murmurs. "Only Lauren."

"I will never believe you again. Never again." He tries to reach his crutches, to stand up, but he is so upset that his leg trembles and he falls back helplessly on to the sofa. "You know what disgusts me most of all? Being dependent on you. I can't even tell you to piss off, I can't even stand up to hit you, to throw your clothes out the window, to kick you outside like the dog that you are. Oh, you're crying now? Go ahead and cry. I've got no tears left. I always hated it when you cried; now it makes me want to gouge your eyes out. What have you done to me? You've turned me into an idiot, a cuckold, a pathetic loser. You know what bothers me most? Your little black notebook. Yeah, the black notebook on your desk. I read what you wrote in there, about how bored you are with this shitty bourgeois life of ours. So not only have you been fucked by half the men in Paris but you despise everything we built. Everything *I* built, working like a dog so that you would have everything you wanted. So you wouldn't have to worry about a thing. Don't you think I want something more than this life too? Don't you think I have dreams, that I wish I could escape? Don't you think I'm also 'romantic,' as you put it? Yeah, go ahead and cry! Cry your fucking eyes out. I don't care how many excuses and explanations you come up with, the truth is you're just a slut, Adèle. You're scum."

Adèle leans against the wall and slides down to the floor. She is sobbing.

"What did you expect, eh? Did you think you could get away with it? That I'd never find out? There's always a price to pay for lying, you know. And you're going to pay. I'm going to hire the best lawyer in Paris, and I'm going to take you for everything you've got. You'll have nothing! And if you think I'm going to let you have custody of Lucien, you're completely nuts. You will never see your son again, Adèle. Trust me on that: you'll be out of his life forever."

Men like to look at their dicks while they're having sex. They support themselves with their arms, lean down, and watch their shaft penetrating the woman. Just to make sure that it's all working properly. They spend a few seconds appreciating this movement, enjoying the simple, efficient mechanics of it. Adèle knows there is a kind of arousal to this self-contemplation. And that it is not only their own genitals that they like to watch, but hers too.

Adèle has spent a long time looking up. She has examined dozens of ceilings, followed the curved lines of moldings, the rocking of lamps. Lying on her back, on her side, her feet resting on the shoulders of a man, Adèle has inspected her surroundings. She has scrutinized the cracks in a painting, spotted water damage; once, she counted the plastic stars in a living room that also served as a child's bedroom. For hours on end she has stared at blank ceilings. Sometimes a shadow, or the projection of a neon sign outside, will divert her attention.

Since Lucien is on vacation now, Adèle spreads out a foam mattress on the lime-tree-lined driveway. She makes a picnic lunch, then they take a nap together in the shade of the trees. Lucien lies next to her and, as he falls asleep, he makes her promise that they will take their nap outside tomorrow too. Her eyes full of the sky, pupils disturbed by the slight movement of leaves, Adèle promises.

"Christine? Christine, can you hear me?" Richard shouts.

The secretary, a blond woman with a face like an albino owl, comes into his office.

"Sorry, Doctor, I was looking for Madame Vincelet's file."

"Could you call my wife for me, please? I haven't been able to get hold of her."

"Should I call your home number, Doctor?"

"Yes, please, Christine. And her cell too."

"Maybe she's gone outside. It's such a lovely day . . ."

"Please call her, Christine."

Richard's office is located on the first floor of the clinic, in the center of town. In the space of a few months Dr. Robinson has won over a large number of regular patients who appreciate his devotion and his competence. He sees patients three days a week and operates on Thursdays and Friday mornings.

It is eleven o'clock on a particularly busy morning. Richard has not yet told the mother of the Manceau boy this, but his symptoms are extremely worrying. Richard has an intuition for things like that. And Mr. Gramont refused to get out of his chair. Even though Richard kept telling him that he wasn't a dermatologist, Mr. Gramont insisted on showing him his moles while claiming that all doctors are thieves and that they wouldn't steal from him.

"She's not answering, Doctor. I left a message asking her to call you back."

"What do you mean, she's not answering? That's not supposed to be possible! Shit!"

The owl rolls her round eyes.

"I didn't know. You didn't tell me . . ."

"I'm sorry, Christine. I slept very badly last night, and Mr. Gramont pushed me over the edge. I don't know what I'm talking about. Please send in the next patient. I'm going to wash my hands."

He bends over the sink and puts his hands under the cold water. His skin is dry and covered with little scabs from being washed. He brings the soap to a lather and rubs his hands frenetically, fingers writhing.

He sits down, his elbows on the armrests

of his chair, his legs outstretched. Slowly he bends his knees. Six months after the accident, his knees still feel rusty. He knows that he still has a slight limp, even if everyone else tells him that it's not noticeable. He walks slowly, awkwardly. At night he dreams that he's running. A dog's dreams.

He is hardly even listening to the patient who sits facing him. A woman in her fifties, anxious, hair tied in a bun to mask her baldness. He asks her to lie down on the examining table and places his hands on her abdomen. "Does that hurt?" He doesn't notice that she looks disappointed when he says: "You're fine. Nothing to worry about."

At three o'clock he leaves the clinic. He drives very fast along the winding road. In front of the house the car skids on the gravel. It takes him two attempts to get out of the car. He draws back then propels himself forward into the garden.

Adèle is lying on the grass. Next to her, Lucien is playing.

"I called you and called you. Why didn't you answer?"

"We fell asleep."

"I thought something had happened to you."

"Of course not."

He holds out his hand and helps his wife to her feet.

"They're coming to dinner tonight."

"Oh, can't you cancel it? It'd be so much nicer with just the three of us."

"No, you can't just cancel at the last minute. It's not done."

"You'll have to take me to the shops, then. It's too far to walk."

She goes into the house. He hears her slam a door.

Richard goes over to his son. He slides his hand through the boy's curly hair, puts a hand on his waist. "Did you stay with Mommy today? What did you do? Tell me." Lucien doesn't answer; he tries to escape from his grasp, but Richard insists. He looks tenderly at his little spy and rephrases the question. "Did you play? Did you do drawings? Lucien, tell me what you did."

Adèle has moved the table into the garden, in the shade of the mirabelle plum tree. She has changed the tablecloth twice and has arranged a bouquet in the center, with flowers picked from the garden. The kitchen windows are open but the air is hot. Lucien is sitting on the ground, at his mother's feet. She gave him a small board and a plastic knife and he is cutting up a boiled zucchini into tiny pieces.

"Is that what you're wearing?"

Adèle is in a blue flower-print dress with thin straps that cross in the back, revealing her shoulders and her thin arms.

"Did you remember my cigarettes?"

Richard takes a packet from his pocket. He opens it and hands a cigarette to Adèle.

"I'll keep the pack here," he says, patting his trousers. "You won't smoke as much that way."

"Thank you."

They sit on the bench outside the kitchen wall. Adèle smokes her cigarette in silence. Lucien carefully replants the boiled zucchini in the ground. They observe the Verdons' house.

Early in the spring a couple arrived on their side of the hill. First, the man came a few times to visit the house. From the window of the little office Adèle could see him in discussion with Emile the gardener, with Mr. Godet the estate agent, and then with various contractors. The man was about fifty years old, very tanned and athletic. He was wearing a bright-colored sweater and what looked like brand-new plastic boots.

One Saturday a truck arrived and parked on the sloping road that the Robinsons had, up to that point, been the only ones to use. Adèle and Richard sat on the bench and watched the couple move into their new house.

"They're Parisians," Richard told her. "They'll only be here on weekends."

He was the one who went to say hello to them, one Sunday afternoon. He led Lucien by the hand and they crossed the road to introduce themselves. He offered to do them a favor: to keep an eye on the house while they were away, and to call them if there was ever a problem. And as he was leaving he invited them to dinner. "Just let me know when you'll be here next. My wife and I would be delighted to see you."

"What do they do for a living?"

"He's an optician, I think."

The Verdons are crossing the road. The woman is holding a bottle of champagne. Richard stands up, puts his arm around Adèle's waist, and waves to them. Lucien clings to his mother's leg. He buries his face in her thigh.

"Hello, you." The woman leans down toward Lucien. "Aren't you going to say hello? My name is Isabelle. What's your name?"

"He's shy," Adèle says apologetically.

"Oh, don't worry about it. I've got three myself, I know what it's like. Enjoy him! Mine refuse to leave Paris. They're not interested in spending the weekend with their old parents anymore."

Adèle goes to the kitchen. Isabelle starts to follow her but Richard pulls her back. "Come and sit down. She prefers to be alone in her kitchen."

Adèle hears them talking about Paris, about Nicolas Verdon's office in the seventeenth arrondissement, and about Isabelle's job in a press agency. She looks older than her husband. She has a loud voice and she laughs a lot. And even though they're in the countryside, in the middle of summer, she is wearing an elegant black silk blouse and a pair of earrings. When Richard tries to pour her a glass of rosé she delicately puts her hand over her glass. "That's quite enough for me. I don't want to be tipsy."

Adèle goes outside to sit with them, Lucien trailing at her heels.

"Richard was telling us that you left Paris for the countryside," says Nicolas enthusiastically. "Quite right! You have everything you need here: earth, stones, trees, real things. I can't wait to retire here."

"Yes. It's a beautiful house."

They look over at the rows of lime trees that Richard planted along the driveway. The sunlight filters through the leaves and spreads a phosphorescent bright-green light over the garden.

Richard talks about his work, about what he calls his "vision of medicine." He tells stories about his patients — funny, moving stories that he has never told Adèle before — and she listens, eyes lowered. She wishes their guests would leave, so the two of them could stay there in the cool of the evening.

So they could finish the bottle of wine on the table, even in silence, even a bit annoyed with each other. So they could walk upstairs, one behind the other, and go to bed.

"Do you work, Adèle?"

"No. But I was a journalist in Paris."

"Don't you miss it?"

"Working forty hours a week to earn the same salary as a nanny?" Richard interrupts. "It's really not worth it."

"Would you give me a cigarette?"

Richard takes the pack from his pocket and puts it on the table. He's had a lot to drink.

They eat unenthusiastically. Adèle is a bad cook. The guests pay her compliments, but she knows that the meat is overcooked, the vegetables tasteless. Isabelle chews slowly, her face tense, as though she is afraid of choking.

Adèle smokes constantly. Her lips are stained blue by the tobacco. She raises her eyebrows when Nicolas asks her, "as a journalist," what she thinks about the situation in Egypt.

She doesn't tell him that she never reads newspapers anymore. That she never turns on the television. That she has even given up watching films. She is too afraid of intrigues, of love, of sex scenes, of naked bodies. She is too nervous to bear the agitation of the world.

"I'm not a specialist in Egypt. *Par contre . . .*"

"*En revanche,*" Richard corrects her.

"Yes, *en revanche,* I have worked quite a lot in Tunisia . . ."

The conversation becomes generic, dull. The silences grow longer. Once they have exhausted all the subjects that strangers can discuss without risk, they find they don't have much to say to one another. The only sounds are of forks scraping plates and food being swallowed. Adèle stands up, a cigarette dangling from her mouth, a plate in each hand.

"It's exhausting, all this fresh air!" The Verdons repeat the joke three times and finally leave, practically pushed out of the garden by Richard, who waves good-bye to them from the gravel driveway. He watches them enter their house, wondering what secrets, what flaws that dull couple might be hiding.

"What did you think of them?" he asks Adèle.

"I don't know. Nice."

"And him? What did you think of him?"

Adèle does not look up from the sink.

190

"I told you. I thought they seemed nice."

Adèle goes up to the bedroom. Through the window she sees the Verdons closing their shutters. She lies down and does not move. She waits for him.

Not once have they slept in separate rooms. At night Adèle listens to his breathing, his snoring, all those guttural sounds that comprise a couple's life. She closes her eyes and curls up very small. With her face at the edge of the bed, her hand dangling over the side, she doesn't dare turn around. She could bend a knee, reach out with an arm, brush his skin as she feigns sleep. But she doesn't move. If she touched him, even accidentally, he might get angry. He might change his mind and throw her out.

When she is sure that he's asleep, Adèle turns over. She looks at him, in the trembling bed, in this room where everything seems to her so fragile. Never again will the slightest gesture be innocent. This terrifies and enraptures her.

Back when he was a junior doctor, Richard did an internship in the emergency room at the Pitié-Salpêtrière hospital. It was the kind of place where you are constantly told that here "you'll learn a lot — about medicine, and about human nature." Richard mostly treated flu cases, people hurt in car accidents, assault victims, and vagus nerve disorders. He had expected to encounter extraordinary cases, but the internship proved deeply boring.

He has a very clear memory of the man who was admitted that night. A tramp, his trousers soiled with shit. His eyes were rolled back in his head, there was froth on his lips and his body was shaken by convulsions. "Is he epileptic?" Richard asked the department head.

"No, he's in withdrawal. Delirium tremens."

When they stop drinking, alcoholics suffer

unbearably violent withdrawal symptoms. "Three to five days after ceasing to drink, the patient suffers vivid hallucinations, often visual and associated with animals such as snakes and rats. The patient is agitated, in a state of extreme disorientation, prone to paranoid delusions. Some hear voices, others have seizures. If untreated, sudden death is possible. As these symptoms are often worse at night, the patient will need company."

Richard watched over that tramp, who banged his head against walls and waved his arms in the air to shoo something away. He administered tranquilizers and prevented the tramp from hurting himself. Calmly he cut off the soiled trousers and rubbed the tramp's skin. He cleaned his face and trimmed his beard, which was thick with dried vomit. He even gave him a bath.

In the morning, when the patient had recovered the few wits that he had left, Richard attempted to explain the situation to him: "You mustn't stop like that. It's very dangerous, as you can see. I know you probably felt like you had no choice, but there are methods, special protocols for people in your condition." The man did not look at him. His face was swollen and purple, his eyes yellowed by jaundice. From time to time he would shudder, as if a rat had just crawled over his back.

After practicing medicine for fifteen years, Dr. Robinson feels confident that he knows the human body. That there is nothing that can deter or frighten him. He is able to detect signs, cross-check clues. Find solutions. He even knows how to measure pain, asking his patients how badly they're suffering "on a scale of one to ten."

With Adèle, he has the feeling that he's been living with a sick person who showed no symptoms, that he was in the presence of a dormant cancer, spreading from cell to cell without declaring itself. When they moved to the new house he kept waiting for her to suffer. To become agitated. He fully expected her to lose her mind, like any other addict deprived of her drug, and he was prepared for this eventuality. He told himself that he would know what to do if she became violent, if she tried to beat him up, if she screamed through the night. If she cut herself, if she stabbed a knife under her fingernails. He would react rationally, scientifically. He would prescribe the right medicine. He would save her.

■ ■ ■ ■

The night he confronted her, he was bereft. He had not made any decision about their future. He just wanted to unburden himself, watch her collapse before his eyes. He was still in shock, and Adèle's passivity infuriated him. She did not attempt to justify herself. She didn't try to deny it. She was like a child, relieved to have her secret discovered and ready to take her punishment.

She poured herself a glass of wine. She smoked a cigarette and said: "I'll do whatever you want." Then she stammered: "Saturday is Lucien's birthday." And he remembered. Odile and Henri were supposed to come to Paris. It had been arranged weeks beforehand, and Clémence, the cousins, and lots of friends were expecting to see them. He didn't have the courage to cancel everything. He knew it was ridiculous, that such a minor social event had no importance compared with the destruction of their marriage, but even so he clung to it as to a piece of driftwood.

"We'll celebrate his birthday and then we'll see." He gave her instructions. She was not to sulk or cry. She had to be cheerful, smiling, perfect. "You shouldn't have any problem with that: you're good at pretending to be something you're not." The idea that someone might find out, that the truth would be revealed, was enough to induce a panic attack in Richard. If he and Adèle were going to split, he would have to come up with an explanation: something simple and believable. Say that they didn't get on anymore. He made her swear not to tell anyone. And never to speak Lauren's name in his presence.

On Saturday he blew up balloons in silence. They decorated the apartment and Richard made a superhuman effort not to yell at Lucien, who was running from room to room like a madman. He didn't reply when Odile expressed surprise that he was drinking so much in the middle of the afternoon. "It's a children's party, isn't it?" she said.

Lucien was happy. At seven in the evening he fell asleep fully clothed, surrounded by his new toys. The two of them were left alone together. Adèle moved toward him, smiling, her gaze luminous. "That went well, didn't it?" Lying on the sofa, he watched her tidy up the living room. Her calmness was monstrous, he thought. He couldn't stand being near her. Everything she did irritated him. The way she swept her hair back behind her ears. The way she dabbed with her tongue at her lower lip. The way she banged the dishes as she washed them in the sink. The way she never stopped smoking. He saw nothing charming or interesting about her. He wanted to beat her, to watch her disappear.

He went up to her and in a firm voice said: "Pack your bags and go."

"What? Now? What about Lucien? I haven't even said good-bye to him."

"Get out of here!" he yelled.

He hit her with his crutches and pushed her into the bedroom. Steely-eyed, without a word, he threw her things into a bag. He went into the bathroom and, with a single hand movement, swept all her toiletries, all her perfume bottles, into a clutch bag. For the first time, she begged him. She went down on her knees. Eyes red with tears, her words torn by gasps and sobs, she swore that she would die without them. That she would not survive the loss of her son. She said she would do whatever it took to be forgiven. That she wanted to get better. That she would give anything for a second chance with him. "That other life meant nothing to me. Nothing." She told him that she loved him. That no other man had ever mattered to her. That he was the only one she could imagine living with.

He had thought he was strong enough to throw her out into the street, without money, without work, with no option but to go back to her parents' seedy apartment in Boulogne-sur-Mer. For a minute or so he even felt he would be able to answer Lucien's questions about her absence. "Mommy is ill. She needs to live far away from us so she can get better." But in the end he couldn't do it. He didn't manage to open the door, to push her out of his life. He couldn't bear the idea that she might exist somewhere else. As if his anger were not enough. As if he needed to understand what had led them both into such madness.

He dropped the bag on the floor. He stared into her pleading eyes, her hunted animal's eye, and he shook his leg to prevent her clinging to it. She fell to the floor and he left. It was bitterly cold outside but he felt nothing. Holding tight to his crutches, he hobbled along the street to the taxi rank. The driver helped him lay his plaster cast on the backseat. Richard handed him some money and asked him to drive. "And turn off the music, please." They kept crossing bridges over the Seine and driving along its banks in an interminable zigzag. They sped along, his pain following close behind. Richard had the feeling that if they stopped moving forward for even an instant he would be crushed by sorrow, incapable of moving a muscle, of breathing. Finally the driver dropped him off near the Gare Saint-Lazare. Richard went into a brasserie. It was full of people: old couples who'd just been to the theater, noisy tourists, divorced women looking for a new life.

He could have called a friend, cried on someone's shoulder. But how could he have told them? What could he have said? Adèle probably believes that it's shame that has stopped him confiding in anyone. That he would rather save face than ask a friend for support and compassion. She must think that he is afraid of the humiliation, of being seen as a cuckold. But he doesn't care what anyone else thinks of him. What he fears is what people will say about her, the way they will stereotype her, reduce her. The way they will caricature his sadness. What he fears the most is that they will force him into a decision, telling him confidently: "In these circumstances, Richard, you have no choice: you must leave her." Talking makes things irreversible.

He didn't call anyone. He just sat there, alone, stared into his glass for hours on end.

He sat there for so long that he didn't even notice the bar emptying. He didn't realize it was two in the morning and that the old waiter in the white apron was waiting for him to pay his bill and leave.

He went home. Adèle was sleeping in Lucien's bed. Everything was normal. Horribly normal. He couldn't believe that he was still able to live.

The next day he delivered his diagnosis. Adèle was sick, and she was going to get better. "We're going to find someone who can help you." Two days later he took her to a medical laboratory, where she gave dozens of blood samples. When he received the results, which were all good, he told her: "You were very lucky."

He asked her questions. Thousands of questions. He didn't give her a minute's respite. He would wake her in the middle of the night to confirm a nagging suspicion, to demand further details. He was obsessed by dates, coincidences, cross-checking facts. She kept repeating: "I don't remember. Honestly, it never mattered to me." But he wanted to know everything about those men. Their names, ages, professions, the places where she met them. He wanted to know how long each affair had lasted, where they had gone, what they had done.

In the end she surrendered and told him everything, lying in the dark, her back turned to him. She was calm and precise, relating the events in a matter-of-fact voice. Sometimes she would start going into sexual details, but he would stop her. "But that's all there was," she said. She tried to explain to him the insatiable desire, the uncontrollable urge, the distress she felt at not being able to put an end to it. But what obsessed him was how she could abandon Lucien for an entire afternoon to meet a lover. How she could invent a professional emergency in order to cancel their family holidays so she could spend two days fucking in a seedy suburban hotel. What simultaneously revolted and fascinated him was the ease with which she had lied to him and led her double life. He felt duped. She had manipulated him like a puppet. Perhaps she even laughed sometimes as she returned to the apartment, leaking semen into her underwear, her skin saturated with another man's sweat. Perhaps she mocked him, imitated him in front of her lovers. He imagined her saying: "My husband? Oh, don't worry about him, he doesn't have a clue."

He stirred up his memories until he felt nauseated. He tried to remember how she had acted when she came home late, when she disappeared. What about how she had smelled? And her breath, when she spoke to him . . . Had it been scented with the breath of other men? He searched for a sign, a clue, perhaps, that he hadn't wanted to see at the time. But no memorable events — nothing at all — came to mind. His wife had been a perfect impostor.

When he'd introduced Adèle to his parents, Odile had had her reservations about her son's choice of partner. She hadn't said anything to him, but Clémence had told him that she'd used the word "calculating." "Adèle is not her idea of a girl. She finds her pretentious." Odile had always been suspicious of that secretive woman. She was worried by her coldness, her lack of maternal instinct.

But he — this student from the provinces, shy and awkward — was dying to hold her in his arms. It wasn't only her beauty that captivated Richard, but her attitude too. He had to take deep breaths whenever he looked at her. Her presence filled him to the point of pain. He loved to watch her live; he knew by heart every little gesture she made. She didn't speak much. Unlike the young women in his medicine classes, she didn't indulge in gossip or trivial conversation. He took her to the best restaurants. He organized trips to cities that she'd always dreamed of visiting. Soon after they met he introduced her to his parents. He asked her to move in with him, and he took care of finding them an apartment. She often said: "This is the first time this has happened to me." And he was proud of that. He promised her that she wouldn't have to worry about anything, that he would take care of her, in a way that no one else ever had. She was his neurosis, his madness, his dream, his ideal. His other life.

"All right. Let's start again."

To start with, she would shut her eyes. That made things impossible. She was so rigid, so cold that it drove him crazy. He wanted to slap her, to stop in the middle of it and leave her there, alone. They do this on Saturday afternoons, sometimes on Sundays. He takes deep breaths when she asks him the same question over and over again in her whiny little-girl voice. She folds her arms, hunches her shoulders, stares straight ahead. She doesn't understand anything.

"Look, just relax," he says, trying not to let his annoyance show. "Don't lean back like that — sit up a little bit. It should be a pleasure, not a kind of torture."

He takes Adèle's hands and places them on the steering wheel. He adjusts the rearview mirror.

One afternoon in July they drive on country roads. Lucien is sitting in the backseat. Adèle is wearing a knee-length dress and her bare feet are on the pedals. It's a hot day and the roads are empty.

"See? There's no one here, so you've got nothing to worry about. You can speed up a little bit, you know."

Adèle turns to look at Lucien, who has fallen asleep. She hesitates, then abruptly steps on the accelerator. The car jumps forward. Adèle is terrified.

"Shift into fourth, for God's sake! You'll wreck the car. Can't you hear that noise? What the hell are you doing now?"

Adèle slams on the brakes and looks sheepishly at Richard.

"It's incredible. It's like you're incapable of using your hands and your feet at the same time. You're really shit at this, you know?"

She shrugs and bursts out laughing. Richard stares at her, speechless. He had completely forgotten the sound of her laughter. That sound like rushing water, like a torrent. That throaty sound she makes when she throws her head back and exposes her long neck. He had forgotten the strange habit she has of putting her hands in front of her mouth and closing her eyes, her face forming a grimace that makes her laughter seem mocking, almost malicious. He has a sudden desire to hold her tight, to feed on this unexpected joy, this cheerfulness that is so absent from their lives.

"I'm going to drive back. And you know what? I think you'd better take some real driving lessons. With a professional, I mean. I think that'll work better."

Adèle makes slow progress, but Richard promises that he will buy her a car if she passes the test. He probably won't be able to stop himself checking the odometer and he'll limit her budget for gas, but at least she'll be able to make small trips on her own. When they moved into the house he would watch her all the time. He couldn't help it. He even followed her around, as if she were a criminal. He would call her several times a day on the house's landline. Sometimes he would leave the clinic on a sudden impulse and drive to the house, between consultations, to find her sitting in her blue chair, staring at the garden.

Sometimes he could be cruel. He would use his power over her to belittle her. One morning she asked him to drop her off in town on his way to the clinic. She felt like walking around town, visiting a few shops. She even suggested they have lunch together, in a restaurant that he had mentioned. "Can you wait for me? I'll just be ten minutes." She went upstairs to get ready. She locked the bathroom door and he left. She must have heard the engine start as she was getting dressed. She probably looked through the window and saw the car disappear. That evening he didn't even mention the incident. He asked her how her day had been. "Very nice," she replied with a smile.

In public he acts in a way that he regrets afterward. He grips her arm, pinches her skin, watches her so closely that the people around them are embarrassed. He examines every movement she makes. He reads her lips. They rarely go out but he is glad that he invited the Verdons. Perhaps they will host a party in September. Something simple, with his colleagues and the parents of Lucien's friends.

He is tired of these constant suspicions. He is sick of thinking that she is only here because of her lack of independence. He promises to leave a bit more money in the house. He encourages her to take Lucien on the train to see his grandparents in Caen or Boulogne-sur-Mer. He has even told her that it's time she started thinking about what kind of job she might like to do.

Sometimes he gives way to an irrational enthusiasm, to an optimism that all doctors are warned to beware. He becomes convinced that he can cure her, that she clung to him because she sensed that he was her savior. Yesterday she woke up in a good mood. It was a beautiful morning. Richard took her into town with Lucien because she had to buy him some things for school. In the car she talked about a dress she'd seen in a shop window, a dress she liked. She began to stammer vaguely about the money she had left and how she was going to save up to buy herself that dress. Richard interrupted her. "Do what you want with the money. You don't have to justify yourself to me." She looked at once grateful and a little disoriented, as if she had become used to the weird game they'd been playing.

"Make her happy." How easy that had sounded when Henri said it about Odile, when he repeated that it was the whole point of life. Start a family and make her happy. How simple that had seemed in the square outside the town hall where they got married, in the maternity ward where Adèle gave birth, at their apartment-warming party, when everyone seemed so sure that Richard possessed all the ingredients for a successful life.

Odile keeps saying that they should have a second child. A house like this, she says, needs a big family. Each time she comes to see them she glances questioningly at Adèle's belly and Adèle shakes her head. Richard is so embarrassed that he pretends not to understand this silent communication.

He imagined a new life for her, one where she would be protected from herself, from her urges. A life composed of habits and constraints. Every morning he wakes her. He does not want her to lie around in bed, brooding. Too much sleep is bad for her. He doesn't leave the house until he has watched her put on her sneakers and start running along the driveway. Out near the hedge she turns to wave at him and then he starts the engine.

Simone has always had a horror of the countryside, probably because she grew up in it. She spoke of it to her daughter as a place of desolation, and in Adèle's eyes nature is a wild beast that we think we have tamed but that can savage us without warning. She doesn't dare say this to Richard, but she is afraid of running on country roads, of penetrating the dark forest. In Paris she liked to run through crowds. The city gave her its rhythm, its tempo. Here she runs more quickly, as if pursued by assailants. Richard would like her to enjoy the scenery, to be awed by the calm of the valleys and the harmony of the landscape. But she never stops running. She runs until her lungs burn and when she gets home she is exhausted, her temples throbbing, amazed and relieved that she didn't get lost. She barely has time to take off her shoes before the telephone rings. She catches her breath before answering Richard's call.

"I have to wear myself out." That's what she thinks, to encourage herself. In the mornings, after a good night's sleep, she can sometimes even believe it. She is capable of optimism, of making plans. But the hours pass, nibbling away at what remains of her determination. Her psychiatrist has advised her to scream. Adèle laughed when he told her that. "No, I'm completely serious. You have to yell, at the top of your voice." He told her it would bring her relief. But even alone, even in the middle of nowhere, she has not managed to express her rage. She has not managed to scream.

In the afternoon she is the one who goes to pick up Lucien. She walks down to the village. She doesn't speak to anyone. She greets passersby with a nod of her chin. The familiarity of the villagers chills her. She avoids waiting outside the school gates for fear that the other mothers will try to talk to her. She explains to her son that he just has to walk a little farther to reach her. "You know, where the statue of the cow is. That's where I'll wait for you."

She always gets there early. She sits on the bench, opposite the covered market. When the bench is occupied she stands next to it, her face impassive, until the person sitting there feels so uneasy that they get up and leave. Richard told her the village was accidentally bombed by the Americans in 1944. In less than twenty minutes the whole place was wiped off the map. The architects attempted to reconstruct the buildings identically, to reproduce the half-timbered Norman style, but the effect is artificial. Adèle asked him if the American planes had spared the church for religious reasons. "No," he answered, "it was just more solid than the other buildings."

When spring arrived her doctor insisted that she spend her days outside. He advised her to take up gardening, to plant flowers that she could then watch grow. Emile helped her dig a vegetable garden at the end of the lawn. She spends a lot of time there with Lucien. Her son likes wallowing in the mud, watering the broad beans, chewing the earth-stained leaves. Even at the start of July she can't help noticing that the days are getting shorter. She watches the sky, which darkens ever earlier, and she feels anxious at the thought of the coming winter. The endless days of rain. The lime trees that will have to be trimmed and that will exhibit their black stumps, like giant corpses. When she left Paris she gave up everything. Now she has no job, no friends, no money. Nothing but this house, where summer is an illusion and winter holds her captive. Sometimes she is like a frightened bird, banging its beak against the bay windows, breaking its wings on the door handles. She finds it ever harder to conceal her impatience, to suppress her irascibility. And yet she does try. She bites the insides of her cheeks, she does breathing exercises to control her anxiety. Richard has forbidden her to let Lucien watch television all day, so she has to invent amusing activities for him. One evening Richard found his wife sitting on the living-room carpet, eyes swollen and red. She had spent all afternoon trying to clean a paint stain that Lucien had left on her blue chair. "He wouldn't listen to me.

He doesn't know how to play," she repeated, her mouth twisted with anger, her knuckles white.

"The last time you came to see me you said you thought you were cured. What did you mean by that?"

"I don't know," she says, with a shrug.

The doctor lets the silence stretch out. He looks at her with his kindly eyes. The first time she saw him in his office he told her he didn't have the resources to treat her. That the usual recommendation was for behavioral therapy: treatment through sport and support groups. In a cold, firm voice she replied: "I'm not doing that. It disgusts me. There's something cowardly about putting your shame on display like that."

She had insisted on continuing to see him instead of finding another psychiatrist. She trusted him, she said. Reluctantly he agreed, moved as he was by the sight of that pale, thin woman in her too-large blue shirt.

"Let's just say that I feel calm."

"That's being cured, for you? Feeling calm?"

"Yes. I suppose. But there's something terrible about being cured too. It means losing something. You understand?"

"Of course."

"At the end, I was scared all the time. I had the feeling that I'd lost control. I was tired. I had to stop. But I never would have believed that he could forgive me."

Adèle's fingernails scratch the cloth armrest of the chair. Outside, black clouds flaunt their pointed nipples. The storm will soon break. From where she sits she can see the side path and the car where Richard waits.

"The night he found out the truth, I slept very well. A deep, soothing sleep. When I woke, even though the house was a wreck, even though Richard hated me, I felt a strange kind of joy, even a sort of excitement."

"Relief."

Adèle says nothing. Rain pours hard on to the cobblestones. The sky is so dark it looks like night has fallen in the middle of the afternoon.

"My father died."

"Oh, I'm sorry to hear that, Adèle. Was your father ill?"

216

"No. He had a stroke last night, in his sleep."

"Does that make you sad?"

"I don't know. He never really liked being here."

She rests her face on her right hand and sinks back into the armchair.

"I'm going to his funeral. On my own. Richard can't leave the clinic and he thinks that Lucien is too young to deal with death. In fact, he hasn't even offered to go with me. I'm going there alone."

"Are you upset with Richard for abandoning you in these circumstances?"

"Oh no," she replies softly. "I'm delighted."

Richard never felt sex was important. Even when he was young it never gave him any great pleasure. He always got a bit bored while he was doing it. It seemed to last a long time. He felt incapable of playing the role of a passionate lover, and — stupidly — he had thought that Adèle would be relieved by the feebleness of his desire. Like any intelligent, sophisticated woman would be. He thought that, compared to all he had to offer her, sex was negligible. In public he would sometimes pretend a little bit, partly for appearances' sake and partly to reassure himself. He would make a vulgar remark about a girl's bottom. He would imply to his friends that he'd had a one-night stand. He wasn't proud of this. The truth was he never thought about sex.

He had always dreamed of being a father, of having a family who would depend on him and to whom he could give everything he had received from his own parents. He had desired Lucien more than anything and he had been anxious at the thought of his conception. But Adèle had become pregnant very quickly — at the first attempt, in fact. He had pretended to be proud of this, to see it as proof of his virility. In reality he was relieved that he didn't have to wear out the body of the woman he loved by "trying" over and over again.

Not once did Richard think of revenge. He didn't even consider attempting to balance things out, in a battle that he knew was lost in advance. He did once have an opportunity with a girl and he took it without really thinking. With no idea of what he was hoping to get out of it.

Three months after he started working at the clinic, he was introduced to Matilda, who was doing an internship at her father's pharmacy. She was a plump young woman with olive eyes, her acne hidden behind her long red hair. She was almost pretty.

One evening Richard was drinking a beer in a bar opposite the clinic when he saw her, sitting with two other women of the same age. She waved at him. She smiled at him. He wasn't sure if she was inviting him to join them or if she just felt obliged to say hello because he was her father's friend. Richard waved back.

He thought no more about it, his brain slowed by alcohol and the heat. He had completely forgotten about her when she walked over to his table and said: "It's Richard, isn't it?"

Drops of sweat trickled down his spine.

"Yes, Richard Robinson." He stood up awkwardly and shook her hand.

She sat down without asking; apparently she was less shy than he had imagined when he saw her blush behind the pharmacy counter. She started talking about university, about Rouen where she was living, about the medical degree she would like to take but for which she did not feel brave enough. She spoke very fast, in a high-pitched, singsong voice. Richard nodded limply, his face slick with sweat. He made an effort to keep his large eyes fixed on her, to smile at the right moments, at times even to rekindle the conversation.

They walked aimlessly through the streets. He asked her for a cigarette, which he struggled to smoke. He felt like asking: "So, what are we doing exactly?" but in the end he said nothing. They walked to the clinic. Outside the building they neither hesitated nor hurried. Richard took the keys from his pocket and they went through the garage.

In his office Richard closed the shutters.

"Sorry, I don't have anything to drink. Some water, if you like?"

"Can I smoke?"

Her skin. Her milky skin was insipid. He put his lips to it. He opened his mouth slightly, licked the hollow of her neck, kissed behind her ear. Her flesh was utterly devoid of any flavor or contour. Even her sweat was odorless. Only her fingers smelled slightly of cigarettes.

She unbuttoned the thin white blouse she was wearing and Richard, aghast, contemplated her round belly, the folds formed by her skirt, the little bulges between the elastic edges of her bra. Adèle's skeleton came back to haunt him.

Matilda looked a little ridiculous, a plump twenty-five-year-old leaning against the desk trying to act like a femme fatale. The room was completely silent. Even the desk didn't squeak. She was hardly breathing. She tried a few things but she seemed disappointed that a forbidden liaison with an older — and married — man did not create more in the way of sparks. It was even less fun than with the boys at the university. Richard was not fun.

She threw her head to one side and then the other. She shut her eyes. Her voluptuous thighs closed around Richard. But even though he gripped her buttocks, undid her bra and stared at her white breasts, he did not manage to come. He withdrew slowly and, once they were out in the street, she rejected his offer to walk her home.

"I live really close anyway."

He took his car. His mind was clear now. On the way home he kept putting his hands to his nose, sniffing and even licking them, but they smelled of nothing more than antiseptic soap.

Matilda had left no trace.

Richard takes her to the train station. In the car Adèle looks through the window. It is just past dawn. Misty sunlight caresses the hilltops. Neither of them gives voice to the strangeness of the situation. She doesn't dare reassure him, act tenderly, promise him that she has no plans to escape. Richard is relieved that the moment has come to let her go, to remove the leash, even for just a few hours, and let her taste freedom.

She will come back.

Outside the station, he looks at her. Beautiful and sad, she smokes her cigarette. He takes out his wallet and hands her a wad of cash.

"Two hundred euros. Will that be enough?"

"Yes, don't worry."

"If you need more, tell me."

"No, thank you. That's fine."

"Put it away now, so you don't lose it."

Adèle opens her handbag and puts the money into one of its pockets.

"See you tomorrow, then."

"Yes. See you tomorrow."

Adèle takes her seat: next to the window, facing backward. The train moves away. A polite silence fills the compartment. Every sound and gesture is muted; people put a hand over their mouth as they talk on the phone. Children sleep. Ears are covered by headphones. Adèle is sleepy and, outside, the landscape becomes a blur of color spilling out of the frame, a half-melted drawing, a flow of gray, an ooze of green and black. She is wearing a black dress and a slightly old-fashioned jacket. Opposite her, a man sits down and says hello. The kind of man she might have hit on in the past. She feels nervous, disoriented. It is not men she's afraid of, but solitude. No longer being watched by anyone, being a stranger, anonymous, a nobody lost in the crowd. Being in movement and thinking that it would be possible to flee. Not that she is considering it, but simply that it is possible.

At the far end of the compartment a girl stands behind the glass door. She can't be more than seventeen. Long, thin adolescent legs and a slight slouch. The boy kissing her has not taken off his backpack, and as he leans over her he looks as though he's going to crush her. Eyes closed, mouths open, their tongues twist around each other relentlessly.

Simone asked her if she would like to say a few words in tribute to her father. Adèle replied that she would rather not. In reality she doesn't know what she could even say about this man whom she barely knew.

His mysteriousness was at the root of her adoration. She thought him decadent, quirky, inimitable. She thought him hand-some. He would speak fervently about freedom and revolution. When she was a child he would show her Hollywood films from the 1960s and tell her repeatedly that everyone should live like that. He would dance with her, and Adèle almost cried once, with joy and surprise, when she saw him lift one foot in the air and pirouette on the point of the other foot to Nat King Cole's "Ballerina." He spoke Italian, or so she believed, at least. He told her that he had once eaten caviar from a spoon with dancers from the Bolshoi Ballet in Moscow, where the Algerian state had sent him to study.

Sometimes, in melancholy moments, he would sing a song in Arabic, the meaning of which he never revealed. He would fly into a rage with Simone, blame her for tearing him away from his roots. He would get angry, make unfair accusations, yell that he had no need for any of this, that he could leave it all behind and go off to live on his own, in a shack somewhere, surviving on bread and black olives. He said he would like to learn to plow fields, sow seeds, return to the earth. That he could have been happy with a simple, peaceful life, like the peasants of his childhood. And that sometimes he even envied them, the way a bird, exhausted after a long flight, might envy an ant. Simone would laugh. A cruel, bluff-calling laugh. And he never left.

Adèle is rocked into a half-sleep by the jolting of the train. She opens her parents' bedroom door and sees the big bed. Her father's body, lying there like a mummy. Feet pointing upward, stiff in the shroud. She approaches and looks at the last visible fragments of his skin. His hands, neck, face. The large smooth forehead, the deep lines at the corners of his lips. She rediscovers those familiar features, the path taken by his smile, the full map of paternal emotions.

She lies on the bed, barely an inch from the body. He is everything to her. For once he cannot disappear or refuse to talk with her. One arm behind her head, her legs crossed, she lights a cigarette. She undresses. Naked, lying next to the corpse, she caresses his skin, presses her body against it. She kisses his eyelids and his gaunt cheeks. She thinks about her father's prudishness, his absolute horror of nudity: his own, and others'. Lying there, dead, at her mercy, he can no longer offer any resistance to her obscene curiosity. She leans over him and slowly unties the shroud.

Gare Saint-Lazare. She gets off the train and walks quickly up Rue d'Amsterdam.

They cut all ties with their life before. A clean, total cut. They left behind dozens of cardboard boxes filled with Adèle's clothes, souvenirs of their travels, even photograph albums. They sold their furniture and gave away their paintings. The day of their departure they looked around the apartment without nostalgia. They handed the keys to the landlord and they set off in the driving rain.

Adèle never returned to the newspaper. She felt too cowardly to offer her resignation and in the end she received a letter that Richard waved in front of her face: "Dismissal for gross misconduct. Dereliction of duty." They do not keep in touch with their Parisian friends, former colleagues, old acquaintances. They find excuses not to have visitors. A lot of people are surprised by their sudden departure, but no one tries to find out what has become of them. As if

Paris itself has forgotten them.

Adèle is nervous. She smokes, standing, staring at the other customers, as she waits for a table on the terrace. A tourist couple get up and Adèle sidles over to take their place. She sees Lauren wave at her from the other side of the street and she looks down at the table, as if she does not feel she has permission to smile or show her happiness.

Lauren sits down with her and talks about Adèle's father, his funeral. She says: "If you'd told me earlier I could have gone with you." She asks about Richard, Lucien, the little village, the house. "So what is there to actually do in that godforsaken hole?" she laughs hysterically.

They bring up old memories, but it's all rather half-hearted. Adèle racks her brain, but she can think of nothing to say. Her mind is a blank. She looks at her watch. She can tell her that she'd better leave, that she doesn't want to miss her train. Lauren rolls her eyes.

"What?" Adèle asks.

"You're making the biggest mistake of your life. Why have you buried yourself in that place? Does it really make you happy, being a provincial housewife?"

Adèle is exasperated by Lauren's insistence, by the way she keeps repeating that

229

her marriage with Richard is a mistake. She suspects the advice is motivated not by friendship but by other feelings. "You're not happy — admit it! Not a woman like you! It's not as if you married him for love."

Adèle smokes and nods silently as Lauren talks. She orders another glass of wine and slowly drinks it. When her friend has exhausted all her arguments, Adèle attacks, cold and precise. She surprises herself by imitating Richard's intonations, repeating the exact words that he uses. She develops her ideas clearly, expresses her feelings in a way that her friend cannot refute. She speaks about the happiness of owning a property, the importance for Lucien of being in contact with nature. She sings the praises of modest pleasures, simple daily joys. She even utters the stupid and unjust words: "People who don't have children just can't understand. I hope one day you'll learn that for yourself." The cruelty of those who know they are loved.

Adèle is late, but she walks slowly from the train station in Boulogne-sur-Mer to her parents' apartment. She walks through the gray, ugly, deserted streets. She has missed the ceremony at the crematorium. It took her a long time to reach the Gare du Nord and she missed her train.

When she rings the doorbell, no one answers. She waits on the front steps of the apartment building. A car stops and Simone gets out, escorted by two men. She is wearing a tight black dress, and a little hat pinned to her bun, with a veil. She has even put on a pair of hideous satin gloves that make creases in her wrinkled wrists. She is not afraid of ridicule in that get-up. She is playing the role of the tearful widow.

They go into the apartment. A waiter puts canapés on a table and the guests quickly surround and devour them. Simone places her hand on the hands that are placed on her. She bursts out in uncontrollable sobs, wails Kader's name. She moans in the arms of old men turned lecherous by grief and alcohol.

She has closed the shutters and the heat is stifling. Adèle drops her jacket on the old black armchair and notices that the shelves have been emptied. Her father's records have disappeared and she can still smell the sickly-sweet odor of Simone's furniture polish. The entire apartment appears cleaner than usual. As if her mother had spent all morning scrubbing the floors, dusting the edges of the photograph frames.

Adèle does not talk to anyone. A few guests try to catch her eye. They speak very loud in the hope that she will join their conversation. They look bored to death, as if they've already said all they have to say and they imagine that she will be able to entertain them. She is repulsed by their wrinkled faces, the sounds made by their weary jaws. She wants to stick her fingers in her ears and shut her eyes, like a sulking child.

The eighth-floor neighbor stares at her. His eyes are gluey; it looks as though a tear is hanging from his eyelid. He is the neighbor so obese that Adèle had trouble locating his penis amid the folds of his belly. His penis was layered with sweat under all that fat, rubbed sore by those enormous thighs. She would go up to his apartment in the afternoons after school. He had a living room and two bedrooms. A large balcony with a table and chairs. And a breathtaking view. He would sit down at the kitchen table, trousers around his ankles, and she would stare out at the sea. "See the English coastline? It's like you could almost touch it." The horizon was clear and flat.

"Didn't Richard come with you?" Simone asks as she leads her daughter into the kitchen. She is drunk.

"He couldn't leave Lucien on his own or abandon the clinic in the middle of the week. He told you that on the phone."

"I'm just disappointed, that's all. I thought he would realize that I was very hurt by his absence. There were lots of people I wanted to introduce to him and this was the ideal opportunity. But apparently . . ."

"Apparently what?"

"Well, since he got his clinic and his big house, apparently we're not good enough for him anymore. He's only been to visit once this year, and he looked like he was holding his breath the whole time. I should have guessed then."

"Stop it, Mom. He's working a lot. That's all."

Simone has placed the white-and-pink porcelain urn next to her collection of hotel matchboxes. It looks like a large biscuit jar or an old English teapot. In a single night her father has moved from the black arm-chair to the living-room shelf.

"I never would have guessed that Dad wanted to be cremated."

Simone shrugs.

"He may not have been religious, but still, it's his culture . . . You shouldn't have done that, Mom. You could have talked to me about it." Adèle's sentence ends in an inaudible murmur.

"Is that why you came? To tell me off? To take your father's side even after his death? It was always all about him. His stupid dreams, his fantasies. 'The high life!' That's what he wanted to live. Our life was never high enough for him. Let me tell you some-thing . . ." Simone swallows a mouthful of gin and clicks her tongue against her inci-sor. "People who are never satisfied destroy everything around them."

The aluminum plates are empty and the guests are saying their farewells to Adèle. "Your mother needs to get some rest." "It was a beautiful ceremony." As they go through the door they all cast a sideways glance at the ashes of her father.

Simone has collapsed on the sofa. She hiccups softly, her makeup smeared over her cheeks. She has taken off her shoes and Adèle looks at her wrinkled skin, covered in brown stains. Her black dress, with a slit up the side, is fastened with a large safety pin. She weeps, grumbling incomprehensibly. She looks terrified.

"You always understood each other. Always ganged up on me. If he hadn't been here you'd never have come to visit, would you? The eighth wonder of the world! Adèle this, Adèle that. It suited him to think that you were still his nice little girl. He always defended you. Too cowardly to punish you, to face up to you. 'Talk to your daughter, Simone!' — that's what he always said. And he turned a blind eye. But you don't fool me. Richard, poor bastard, he doesn't see a thing. He's like your father, blind and naive. Men don't know who we are. They don't want to know. But I'm your mother, I remember everything. The way you wiggled your hips . . . You weren't even eight. You scared men. The grown-ups used to talk about you when you weren't around. And they didn't say nice things, believe me. You

235

were the kind of kid that grown-ups don't like. You had wickedness in you, even then. And you looked like butter wouldn't melt! A perfect little hypocrite, you were. You can leave, you know. I don't expect anything from you. And that poor Richard, who's such a nice man. You don't deserve him."

Adèle puts her hand on Simone's wrist. She wishes she could tell her the truth. Could confide in her and depend on her goodwill. She would like to caress her forehead, where a few fine curls stick to the skin, like a child's hair. She was a burden to her mother when she was a child. Now she has become an adversary, without ever having the time for tenderness, for gentleness, for explanations. She doesn't know where to start. She is afraid that she will say the wrong thing, cracking the shell and releasing thirty years of bitterness. She does not want to witness one of those hysterical fits that punctuated her childhood: her mother, face covered in scratches, hair disheveled, screaming abuse at the entire world. Adèle swallows, says nothing.

Simone, numbed by tranquilizers, falls asleep with her mouth open. Adèle drinks what remains of the bottle of gin. She downs a glass of white wine that her mother left near the oven. She opens the shutters and looks through the window at the empty parking lot, the little garden with its sun-burned grass. In the squalid apartment where she grew up, she staggers around, bumping into walls. Her hands shake. She wishes she could sleep, tame the rage inside her, but it is still bright outside; it is still early evening as she leaves the apartment, swaying unsteadily. She left an envelope on the sideboard in the entrance hall, along with the orange box containing the brooch.

She takes the bus to the city center. It is a pleasant evening and the streets are full of people. Tourists take selfies. Youngsters drink beer, sitting on the cobbles. She counts her steps to prevent herself falling. She sits on a terrace, in the sun. A little boy sitting on his mother's lap blows through his straw, making bubbles in his glass of cola. The waiter asks Adèle if she's waiting for someone. She shakes her head. She can't stay there. She gets up and walks to a bar.

She has been here before. The tables on the mezzanine, the sticky countertop, the little stage at the back of the room . . . all of this seems familiar. Unless it's just that the place is so horribly banal. The bar is full of noisy, unremarkable students, happily cele-brating their exam results, the start of the summer holidays. Adèle does not belong here, and she senses that the barman is watching her suspiciously, that he has noted her shaking hands, her vacant gaze.

She drinks her beer. She is hungry. A boy sits next to her. A thin young man with a gentle face. The sides of his head are shaved and the hair on top is long and slicked back. He talks a lot but she can barely hear him. She gathers that he is a musician. That he works as a caretaker in a small hotel. He talks about his child too. A baby, just a few months old, who lives with its mother in a town whose name Adèle immediately forgets. She smiles but she is thinking: strip me naked and put me on the bar. Hold my arms, stop me from moving, press my face against the countertop. She imagines the men taking turns, shoving their dicks inside her, flipping her over and fucking her again until they have driven out the sorrow, until they have silenced the fear that lurks deep inside her. She wishes she didn't have to say anything, that she could offer herself like those girls she has seen in Paris, their camel-like eyes staring out from the windows of hostess bars. She wishes the whole bar would drink body shots from her skin, that they would spit on her, that they would reach into her guts and rip them out, until she is nothing but a shred of dead flesh.

They leave the bar by the back door. The boy rolls a joint and hands it to her. She is euphoric and despairing. She begins sentences that she doesn't finish. She keeps repeating: "I've forgotten what I was going to say." He asks her if she has any children. She thinks about her jacket, which she left on the chair in her mother's living room. She is cold. She should go back to the apartment, but it's so late and the apartment seems so far away. She would never dare walk all the way there on her own. She should gird her loins, weigh up the pros and cons, act like a grown-up.

When Richard found out the truth, she imagined that she would end up coming back here, to this town, to her parents' apartment. Humiliated, penniless, with no other options. She shuddered at the idea of going back there and sleeping at the end of the hallway, of hearing her mother's rasping voice attacking and interrogating her, hour after hour. She saw herself hanging from the false ceiling of her bedroom, her high heels dangling from the ends of her toes, her eyes full of that blue-and-white wallpaper that even now gives her nightmares. Her lips violet, her body as light as a feather, she would sway over the little bed, her shame finally extinguished.

"What?"

Why is this boy so desperate to make conversation? She moves closer to him, kisses him, rubs her breasts against his torso, but she finds it hard to stay upright. He catches her as she's falling and laughs. She closes her eyes. The joint has made her nauseated and the floor has started to pitch and roll.

"I'll be back."

She walks across the room, taking deep breaths. In the toilets a group of adolescent girls squeezed into miniskirts are doing their makeup. They giggle. Adèle lies down and raises her legs. She wishes she had the strength to go to the station, to catch a train or throw herself under one. More than anything in the world she wants to return to the hills, to the half-timbered house, to the vast solitude, to Lucien and Richard. She weeps, her cheek sticking to the tile floor with its stink of urine. She weeps because she can't go home.

She stands up. Splashes cold water over her face. In the mirror she looks like a drowned woman. The livid complexion, the bulging eyes, the bloodless lips. She goes back into the bar, where no one notices her. She feels as if she is floating through thick fog. A group of drunk teenage boys jumps up and down, arms around one another's shoulders, yelling out the words of a song.

The boy taps her on the shoulder and startles her.

"Hey, where were you? Are you all right? You're white as a sheet." He gently places his hand on her frozen cheek.

Adèle smiles. A sweet, moved smile. She likes this song. "You give your hand to me . . ." She falls into his arms, abandoning herself to the rhythm of the music. He squeezes her ribs, presses her tight against him, and rubs his hands over her bare arms to warm her up. She puts her cheek on his shoulder. Her eyes are closed. Their feet move slowly as they sway from side to side. He takes her hand and she opens her eyes when he gently spins her around and pulls her back toward him. She smiles and she hums, her lips touching his neck.

"Well, you don't know me . . ."

The song ends. The crowd yells when a faster track starts up. They invade the dance floor. Adèle and the boy are separated. Hands behind her neck, eyes closed, she dances. Her hands move down her body, caress her breasts, converge on her groin.

She lifts her arms, swept along by the accelerating beat of the music. She swings her hips, shakes her shoulders, moves her head from side to side. A wave of calm surges through her. She has the feeling that she is cut off from the world, that she is experiencing a moment of grace. She rediscovers the pleasure she used to feel as a teenager, when she would dance for hours, sometimes alone on the dance floor. Innocent and beautiful. She never felt any embarrassment then. Never worried about the danger. She gave herself over completely to what she was doing, on the cusp of a future that she imagined glorious, higher, greater, more exhilarating. Richard and Lucien are no more than vague memories now, impossible memories that she sees slowly dissolve then disappear.

She spins around, indifferent to the dizziness. Eyes half-closed, she spots little bursts of light in the dark room that help her maintain her balance. She wishes she could dive into the heart of this solitude but they tear her away from it, they drag her toward them, they won't let her. Someone grabs her from behind and she rubs her buttocks against his erection. She does not hear the raucous laughter. She does not see the looks on the faces of the men who pass her between them like a parcel, who press her body against theirs, who laugh at her. She laughs too.

When she opens her eyes, the gentle boy has vanished.

He was waiting on the platform. She wasn't on the 3:25 train. Nor on the 5:12. He called her mobile. She didn't answer. He drank three coffees, bought a newspaper. He smiled at two patients, here to catch a train, who asked him who he was waiting for. At seven o'clock Richard leaves the station. He is in a panic, barely breathing. All he can think about is why Adèle has not come back.

He returns to the clinic but the waiting room is empty. No emergencies to keep his mind occupied. He goes through a few files but he is too nervous to work. He can't imagine spending the night without her. He can't believe that she won't come back. He calls his neighbor and lies: he says there's been an emergency, could she please stay a bit later to look after Lucien?

He walks to the restaurant where some friends are waiting for him. Robert, the dentist. Bertrand, the business manager. And Denis, whose exact occupation no one seems to know. Until now Richard has always avoided groups of friends. He has never been gregarious. Even as a medical student he kept himself to himself. He never took part in the salacious humor of locker rooms. He didn't enjoy hearing his colleagues boast about how they'd slept with a nurse. He was repulsed by that facile, vain male complicity that always seems to revolve around the conquest of women.

It is a hot evening and his friends are waiting for him on the terrace. They've already had a few bottles of rosé and Richard orders a whiskey to catch up. He is nervous, impatient, on a short fuse. He feels like picking a fight with someone, letting his rage explode. But his friends are too boring and placid to get into an argument. Robert talks about the expenses of running a business and asks Richard to back him up. "It's true, isn't it? They're strangling us!" Bertrand, in a calm and condescending voice, gives a long-winded speech about the necessity for solidarity, without which the French social model would fall apart. And Denis — kind, gentle Denis — repeats: "But in fact

245

you're saying the same thing. You're both right."

By the end of the meal Richard's jaw is trembling. The alcohol has made him sad and sensual. He wants to cry, to cut short all conversations. His cell phone lies on the table in front of him and he jumps whenever the screen lights up. She doesn't call. He leaves the table before the digestifs arrive and Robert makes a remark about Adèle's beauty, about Richard's impatience to get home. Richard smiles and winks at him, then leaves the restaurant. He could just as easily have slammed his fist into that boor's thick-lipped face. As if there were some kind of glory in going home to mount his wife.

The road is slippery and he drives fast. It's a warm, stormy night and the thunder makes horses whinny in the distance. He parks the car in the driveway and sits there, looking at the house. The worm-eaten window frames. The wooden bench and the breakfast table. The hills, at whose center the house nests. He chose this house for her. Adèle has not had to worry about a thing. The shutter that used to bang during the night, he had it fixed. He planted the lime trees on the little terrace.

He starts making wagers with himself, the

way he used to do as a child. He promises. He swears that, if she comes back, everything will be different. He won't leave her alone anymore. He will break the silence that pervades this house. He will pull her toward him, he will tell her everything, and then he will listen to her. He will abandon all his bitterness and regrets. He will act as if nothing happened. He will smile and say, "Did you miss your train?," then he will talk about something else and it will all be forgotten.

He is wary of illusions these days, but of one thing he is sure: Adèle has never been as beautiful as she is now. Ever since they left Paris she has had this astonished expression on her face, a humble, softer look in her eyes. No more dark rings. And her eyes have grown larger. Her eyelids are as big as dance floors. At night she sleeps peacefully. A sleep without secrets or intrigues. She says she dreams of a cornfield, a suburban neighborhood, a children's park. He doesn't dare ask her: "Do you still dream of the sea?"

He never touches her but he knows every inch of her body. Every day he examines her. Her knees, her elbows, her ankles. Adèle does not have bruises anymore. He inspects her skin but it's smooth, as pale as the walls of the village. She has nothing to say. Adèle no longer bangs into headboards. Her back no longer gets carpet burns. She no longer wears her hair over her forehead to hide the bumps there. Adèle has put on weight. Beneath her summer dresses he can tell that her bottom is rounder, her belly heavier, her skin less taut, easier to grasp.

Richard wants her. All the time. A violent, selfish desire. Often he wishes he could reach out to her with his hand but instead he just stands there, stupid and immobile. He puts his hand over her vulva, the way you might place your palm over the mouth of a child who is about to scream.

And yet he wishes he could sob into her breasts. Cling to her skin. Put his head in her lap and let her console him for his great, betrayed love. He desires her, but he hears. The comings and goings of the men who have walked over her. This revolts him, obsesses him. That coming and going, that back and forth that does not want to end, that leads nowhere, those skins colliding, those flabby thighs, those revolted looks. That back and forth, regular as blows, like an impossible quest, like the desire to wrest a cry from her, a sob that sleeps deep inside her and that will make the landscape tremble. That back and forth that can never be entirely reduced to itself, that is always the promise of another life, the promise of beauty, of possible tenderness.

He gets out of his car and walks to the house. Drunk and slightly nauseated, he sits on the bench. He searches his pockets for a pack of cigarettes. He doesn't have any. He always smokes hers. She can't leave. She can't abandon them. You can't betray the one who's forgiven you. He sniffs as he thinks that he is going to enter this house alone, that he will have to answer Lucien when he asks: "Where's Mommy? When is she coming home?"

He will go and find her, wherever she is hiding. He will bring her back. He will never let her out of his sight again. They will have another child, a little girl, with her mother's eyes and her father's solid heart. A little girl who will keep her occupied, whom she will love more than anything in the world. Maybe one day she will even be content with the banal preoccupations of an ordinary life and he will be happy, so happy he could die, when she wants to redecorate the living room, when she spends hours choosing new wallpaper for the baby's room. When she talks too much, when she has a tantrum.

Adèle will age. Her hair will turn white. She will lose her eyelashes. No one will see her anymore. He will hold her wrist. He will rub her face in everyday life. He will lead her in his wake, will never let go of her, when she is afraid of the emptiness and wants to fall. And one day he will plant a kiss upon her cracked skin, her parchment cheek. He will undress her. He will no longer hear in his wife's vagina any other echoes but the blood that pulses there.

And she will surrender. She will rest her tremulous head on his shoulder and he will feel the full weight of a body that has thrown down its anchor. She will scatter sprays of funeral flowers over him, and as she nears death she will become more tender. Adèle will rest tomorrow. And she will make love, her bones creaking, her spine rusted. She will make love like a poor old woman, who still believes in it and who closes her eyes and says nothing at all.

This doesn't end, Adèle. No, this doesn't end. Love is only patience. A pious, fanatical, tyrannical patience. An unreasonably optimistic patience.

We're not finished.

ABOUT THE AUTHOR

Leila Slimani is the bestselling author of *The Perfect Nanny,* for which she became the first Moroccan woman to win France's most prestigious literary prize, the Goncourt. She won the La Mamounia Prize for *Adèle.* A journalist and frequent commentator on women's and human rights, she is French president Emmanuel Macron's personal representative for the promotion of the French language and culture. Born in Rabat, Morocco, in 1981, she now lives in Paris with her French husband and their two young children.